Forward from Clapham South

FORWARD FROM CLAPHAM SOUTH

Michael Phillips

The Book Guild Ltd.
Sussex, England

This book is a work of fiction. The characters and situations in this story are imaginary. No resemblance is intended between these characters and any real persons, either living or dead.

This book is sold subject to the condition that it shall not, by way of trade or otherwise, be lent, re-sold, hired out, photocopied or held in any retrieval system, or otherwise circulated without the publisher's prior consent or otherwise circulated in any form of binding or cover other than that in which this is published and without a similar condition including this condition being imposed on the subsequent purchaser.

The Book Guild Ltd.
25 High Street,
Lewes, Sussex.

First published 1990
© Michael Phillips 1990
Set in Baskerville
Typesetting by Southern Reproductions (Sussex),
East Grinstead, Sussex.
Printed in Great Britain by
Antony Rowe Ltd.,
Chippenham, Wiltshire.

British Library Cataloguing in Publication Data
Phillips, Michael
  Forward from Clapham South
  I. Title
  823'.914 [F]

ISBN 0 86332 507 6

For Betty,
who likes this story

1

Barbara was sitting at her typewriter, as she did for several hours a day, five days a week for forty-eight weeks a year. Her job was not very interesting, not very difficult and not very demanding; in the current jargon, the job satisfaction for her was almost non-existent. On this particular Monday morning, she was feeling depressed. She did not make a habit of being gloomy; but it had been her twenty-ninth birthday the day before and, for the first time for ages, she had taken stock of her life so far. Perhaps, she thought, that had been a silly thing to do because it had made her realize that the years were going by, and her life, such as it was, with them. She had given up hoping for much. Perhaps that was why she was such an efficient secretary, concentrating on her work and not being a nuisance to anybody – all very admirable, no doubt, but not very inspiring.

If Barbara had known what was going on at that very moment in a solicitors' office in Lincoln's Inn, she would not have connected it with herself or have guessed that it could change her whole future, if only she would allow it to do so. But she did not know until much later, and so, distracted for once by her feeling of sadness, she ripped a half-typed letter from her machine and, with a half suppressed 'Damn the thing,' she tore it up and started again. It was, as always, a dull letter anyway.

James Garton, sitting in his comfortable office in Lincoln's Inn, had never heard of Barbara. Unlike her, he was feeling elated, because, at an unusually early age, he had just become a partner in the firm. This morning, however, his general happiness was mixed with a little trepidation because he was about to interview his first client in that firm – a Mr Thomas Lindley. James was trying to discover something about Mr

Lindley before the interview by asking the senior partner, Henry Wharton.

'What is Mr Lindley like?'

'What exactly do you wish to know, James?'

'He wants to make a new will. I don't want my very first consultation to go awry. Is my client, despite his age, of sound mind and testamentary disposition?'

James knew that Henry Wharton would be pleased with the technical phrase.

'Very much so,' said Henry. 'You need have no fears on that score. He is physically competent too. He'll walk into your room all by himself, unaided except by a heavy stick, and he'll explain to you very clearly what his wishes are.'

'Well, that's something, I suppose. Just a routine sort of will then?'

'I did not say that,' Henry replied, 'or indeed anything that could be construed as bearing that interpretation. You did not ask me a question clearly intended to elicit information on that subject.'

Getting facts out of Henry reminded James of the phrase 'getting blood from a stone', but it was not quite the right metaphor. Henry had the information, but unless James asked exactly the right question he would not get the answer he wanted.

'Well, is it?' he asked with slight exasperation.

'Is it what?'

'Here we go again,' James thought, but, tactfully, he did not say it. His first client, however eccentric, would present few problems compared with dealing with the senior partner.

'Is it probable,' James rephrased the question, 'that this will be a matter of preparing a simple will?'

'Most improbable,' Henry replied with an enigmatic smile. 'Excuse me.' With that, he promptly disappeared in the direction of his own room. James sat down at his desk and leafed through a text book on wills. His client was, after all, not a typist on board *The Lusitania* whose unfortunate death had given rise to a court case about her will – why did textbooks all give such peculiar and unlikely examples?

Indeed, James was relieved rather than alarmed when his secretary came in to announce the arrival of his client.

'He's exactly on time, Helen,' he said, 'show him in,

please.'

A tall, distinguished looking gentleman was ushered in with considerable deference. James did his best to emanate an air of confidence, which was true, and of experience, which was not.

'Hm!' said the old gentleman. 'New aren't you?'

So much for the attempt to look experienced.

'Yes, sir,' said James. He hoped that the 'sir' did not strike the wrong note; but he felt that as the difference in their ages was so apparent, his use of the word would sound courteous rather than apologetic or tentative.

'Well. No harm in that,' Mr Lindley admitted.

'I hope not.'

'Might, in fact, be a good thing.'

'Yes?'

'Don't like lawyers,' said Mr Lindley.

'Sorry to hear that,' said James, 'but you have come to see one. How can I help you?'

'Hm!' said Mr Lindley once again, sounding more like a retired colonel every minute. 'New one.'

'Perhaps you would like to discuss your new will in general terms first,' James suggested, 'and then I – that is we – can consider the details separately afterwards.'

'Certainly. Rather an odd will, I suppose.'

'Well, I don't know anything about it yet,' James said, quite reasonably, he thought.

'Don't know anything about wills?' Mr Lindley barked.

First his senior partner and then this irascible old gentleman seemed determined to misunderstand him this morning.

'I did not say that,' James hurriedly reassured him. 'Certainly I know a good deal about wills. All I meant was that, as yet, I don't know anything about your wishes as regards this particular will.'

'See, sorry.'

There followed a pause which lasted exactly ten seconds, but it seemed as many minutes to James. Indeed, he was just beginning to wonder whether he ought to break the silence, before his client barked again, when Mr Lindley said, in quite a normal voice,

'My niece, Barbara.'

'Yes?' James tried to sound encouraging. Mr Lindley was remarkably staccato.

'Want to do something for her.'

'Do you want to leave her a simple legacy or the whole or part of your residuary estate?'

'Just a legacy, a big one. That will make her sit up and take notice.'

'Quite so,' said James, as formally as he could. (Henry Wharton would certainly have said that). 'Can you give me some idea of the amount?'

Mr Lindley became silent for a time; and as James already knew the approximate size of the estate, he was about to speak again when Mr Lindley replied, 'Fifty thousand or thereabouts.'

James made a note on his pad.

'Any other legacies?' he asked.

'No. No other relatives. Leave the rest to charities, I suppose.'

James and his client spent a few moments selecting four charities which would share the bulk of the estate between them. They then decided who would be executors and trustees; one of them, of course, was to be James himself.

Nothing so very odd about this will, after all.

'It will give you a great deal of work,' said Mr Lindley.

'I don't suppose so. The provisions of your will seem to be quite straightforward.'

'Ah! But they are not.'

Mr Lindley gave a sphinx-like smile.

'Have you something special in mind, sir?'

Perhaps there was a hidden trap in this apparent simplicity.

'Well, yes.'

There was another lengthy pause. Mr Lindley seemed to specialize in them.

Finally, he said, 'Wanted to be a sheep farmer, you know, in Australia.'

James' mind boggled.

'Your niece, you mean wanted to be a sheep farmer in Australia?'

'No, no, no,' the old gentleman growled, 'I did.'

Was he really as sane as he seemed? James could think of

nothing brighter to say than, 'Oh. Really?'

After another of his characteristic pauses, Mr Lindley added, 'Look. We don't know one another and so we have been a bit formal so far. I want the legacy to my niece to be a sort of treasure hunt and I can explain what I have in mind best if I just talk about it.'

James' mind went back to his text book on wills. 'Treasure hunt,' he thought. Whatever did his client really want? And it had all seemed so simple at first.

'Certainly, Mr Lindley,' he said, trying to sound more confident than he felt. 'Just tell me in your own words what ideas you have on the subject and I'll try to make legal sense of it.'

'It makes sense already,' said his client, somewhat testily.

'I don't doubt it, sir; but you will appreciate that I have not yet heard your ideas in detail.'

With the aid of a glass of sherry, Mr Lindley seemed more prepared to explain what he had in mind.

'When I was a young man,' he began, 'I had a chance of emigrating to Australia to become a sheep farmer. Barbara, my niece, is little more than a shorthand-typist. Secretary? Bah.'

James looked down at his pad. This seemed a very strange beginning. What connexion was there between a potential Australian sheep farmer and a shorthand-typist, who may or may not be a secretary? And where did a treasure hunt come into the picture? It sounded like a conundrum set for 'Round Britain Quiz.' He waited for the old gentleman to elucidate.

'Let me tell the story in my own way,' Mr Lindley recommenced, 'and you can see how best to put it into my will. I am thinking about adventures. When I was a young man, I was always thinking about them; but there was a difference then. When I was young, I was thinking about adventures that I was going to have – or so I thought. Now, it's about adventures that I might have had if I had had the courage, sheep farming, for instance.'

He took another sip of sherry.

'The chance came to me and I let it go. Regretted it ever since. So I became a successful business man in Birmingham;

pots of money but no adventures. Married, but had no children; I'm a widower now. When this niece came along, I was delighted at first – substitute child, don't you know? She's grown up now; much too grown-up. At least I used to think about adventures. She does not even do that, so far as I can see. She was born an adult, I think. Not entirely her own fault. Very repressive parents. So, she's a shorthand-typist. All right as far as it goes, I suppose; but, and this is where it is not all right, she seems content to go on being a shorthand-typist until she gets a pension book.'

Clearly, Mr Lindley had not talked so much for ages and he paused for breath.

'So,' he continued, 'I'm not just giving Barbara fifty thousand pounds. I'm giving her a chance to take some risks. That's what I mean by a treasure hunt.'

'Would you give me some details of this treasure hunt of yours?' James requested.

'Certainly. Worked it all out. Here are the clues.'

He handed to James a large manilla envelope. 'And here,' he paused, 'will you keep the answers secret until she has solved them?'

James, still somewhat bemused, nodded.

'In that case,' said Mr Lindley, producing with the air of a conjuror another large envelope, 'here are the answers.'

James did not quite know what to say to all this.

'If Miss Barbara Lindley agrees to accept the rules,' he asked, 'she will have to prove that she is adventurous. Is that right?'

'Certainly, it is right,' said the old man.

'But how could she possibly afford to have these adventures of yours?'

'Of hers,' his client interrupted, 'but I suppose they will be mine by proxy, don't you know.'

'Very well,' agreed James, 'they will be her adventures. How can she afford the time to set out on them without giving up her present job?'

'Don't see how she could. That is part of the idea.'

'But,' said James, 'if your are asking her to undertake some journeys away from home – which I suppose is what you have in mind, although I have not yet had an opportunity to examine the clues in detail – could you not perhaps arrange for her to have some money to start with?'

'Yes, of course. Hadn't thought of that. Stupid of me. I expect she has got some savings; but I am not asking her to break into those. Look, word the will so that she will get two thousand pounds to start with if she agrees to have a go; and then up to say five thousand pounds for expenses and things if she really gets started on all this.'

'I think I can arrange all that,' said James a little hesitantly. 'I take it that I can examine the clues myself before drafting the will?'

The old man paused. 'Yes, but not at the answers until she has taken the clue. I suppose that you will have to look at the clues to see that they are not illegal; although I can't begin to think why they should be; she won't have to steal The Crown Jewels or anything like that.'

Although James had not supposed anything so wildly improbable as that, he was a trained lawyer and did not like the idea of doing anything in the dark. He realized that he ought perhaps to be worried about something else. The will would include the usual provision that a professional trustee could charge for his services, but it was beginning to look as though he was letting himself in for a considerable amount of unpaid work, which could hardly be described as professional. Was the administration of a treasure hunt part of a trustee's business? However, James was not unduly concerned about money; and this just might be fun.

'I don't yet know your niece, Mr Lindley,' he said at last, 'but if you will forgive me for asking, do you think that it is likely that she will agree to all this?'

'Don't know myself; but I have sometimes had the feeling that there is some sort of explosion lurking behind the surface of her sedate manner. This will give her a chance to explode if she feels like it. Pity I shall not be here to see it.'

2

Three months later, towards the end of March, 1980, Thomas Lindley, dreaming of the adventures that he had never had, died peacefully in his sleep. A week or so after that, Barbara Lindley came back to her little flat in South Battersea to find, on her mat, a letter from his solicitors.

Barbara did not open the letter straight away. She did not receive many letters, not even those in typed envelopes, which were not usually very interesting; so, as she normally did on such comparatively rare occasions, she decided to savour it unopened until after she had prepared her small supper. She made a pot of tea and an egg dish, turned the radio on low and sat down at the table. At the end of the meal but with some tea left in the pot, she picked up the letter. It was probably, she thought, an unwanted advertisement – for double glazing most likely – but there was nevertheless some slight feeling of expectation before opening any letter, a hope that was normally abruptly dashed two seconds later. Perhaps that was why she always deferred the moment. But, on this occasion, for the first time for years, this letter did contain a surprise.

Dear Miss Lindley,
   As you will perhaps be aware, your great-uncle, Thomas Seymour Lindley recently died.

Barbara did not in fact know this; so she broke off for a minute to think about her uncle and felt a little ashamed that she did not feel like bursting into tears. She resumed her reading.

He has left a most unusual will under which you MAY benefit. I am anxious not to raise your hopes unnecessarily; so I will add that the will includes a conditional legacy in your favour. I am afraid that if you do not comply with the condition, you will not receive the legacy.

Your late great uncle specifically asked me to see you in order to explain the condition and to discuss it with you. I shall also be permitted to give you (with certain exceptions) what help I can by way of elucidation. I must also point out that you can demand to see the will in the first instance before seeing me, if that is what you would prefer.

However, if you could find it convenient to call to discuss the matter, perhaps you would kindly telephone to arrange a meeting. Please ask for Mr Garton. I should perhaps add that, for some reason, my late client expressly wished that neither you nor your mother, should be informed of his death until after the funeral.

Yours faithfully,

Squiggle, Squiggle and Squiggle.

Barbara read and re-read this extraordinary epistle. Something, something conditional at any rate, had actually happened at long last. She had had a more than usually irritating day at the office. Fancy having to re-type two long letters, just because each contained an unimportant error; but her new boss was a most inconsiderate man. She had felt tired and dispirited when she arrived home, with nothing to look forward to except a visit to a theatre at the end of the week with her friend Edna. Life was dull and nothing interesting ever happened to Barbara, or so she had thought. She was pleased with her flat, of course; everything was so neat and tidy, just as she liked it. But nothing had ever really happened. She read the letter once again. Something had happened or, at least it could happen if she agreed to this mysterious condition. Whatever could it be? Thinking back about the little she knew about wills, she could recall reading of only one condition – the adoption of a new name. She already had the same surname as her great uncle – or did it have something to do with the unexpected Seymour?

Barbara felt so cheered by the letter, while feeling a little guilty at not being upset by her uncle's death, that she made herself a second pot of tea – a great treat – and day-dreamed for a while. She had, she thought, given up day-dreaming. It had never got her anywhere. She never did go anywhere, except for days or evenings out with Edna and a fortnight's holiday with her at Frinton-on-Sea every September. Even Barbara had begun to rebel about that; but Edna had replied: 'Well, why not? We know that we like Frinton, don't we? If we tried somewhere else, we might find that we didn't like it.'

Irrefutable logic; Barbara could not think of a convincing come-back. Barbara had worked in the same firm for nine years, ever since getting her diploma, with honours, at the secretarial college, so she knew that she would have no great difficulty in getting an afternoon off to see these solicitors.

While Barbara was musing on the strange turn of events, she happened to glance at the looking-glass.

> 'Mirror, mirror on the wall
> Who is the fairest of them all?'

Not me, Barbara wryly admitted to herself. Then she had a surprise, but could not at first realize why. Then it dawned on her. For the first time for weeks, she was feeling happy. So that was what was making her eyes sparkle. Feeling rather foolish, she went nearer to the mirror and had a good look. It was years since she had done anything like that. 'What's wrong with me,' she thought wryly, 'is that I look like other people.' And then she smiled, and it transformed her. 'Very well then,' she decided, 'maybe I have an ordinary face but my hair does curl all by itself and I do have blue eyes.'

Barbara retreated from the mirror, feeling strangely embarrassed. She had almost spoken her thoughts out loud. In any case, fancy peering at herself in such detail in a mirror like that. Thank goodness nobody had seen. But there was, as usual, nobody else in the flat.

Three days later, after her usual very ordinary little lunch, she set off on the first stage of her great adventure.

'But you must not hope for too much,' she told herself repeatedly. 'It may be a horrid condition that I could not possibly agree to.'

She began to wish that she had postponed the interview for a week; it would have given her another few days of hoping. Perhaps today would be the end of her beautiful dream. Something vague and undefined was sometimes the most attractive.

She was always a very punctual young woman and arrived in good time for the meeting. She really enjoyed the feeling of freedom while she wandered around the pleasant district in the warm afternoon sun. Nobody could ring her up and instruct her to take a letter. There was something about Lincoln's Inn that cut it off from the world. It seemed very odd that it was only a few minutes from the buzz and hum of London traffic. The whole thing was very like a dream, but a very clear and colourful one. Barbara was actually looking at the buildings and the well mown lawns instead of charging along, as she usually did, from place to place without really seeing anything.

Exactly on the dot of three, she rang the bell and, with some trepidation, she followed the chic girl who received her into the solicitors office. When she first saw James Garton, she had a pleasant surprise. He was about her own age and very good-looking. Barbara realized that it had been very illogical of her to assume that he would be at least fifty. After all, solicitors do not arise fully armed, with knowledge presumably, from the teeming brain of Minerva – a curious phrase that had stuck in Barbara's mind ever since a Latin lesson so many years ago. But she had not for a moment imagined that James, or 'Mr Garton' as she thought of him then would be a day younger than fifty.

'Do sit down, Miss Lindley,' he said. He had a charming smile.

'Your great-uncle,' he began, 'has left a most unusual will. I don't quite know how best to explain the terms of it to you. The difficulty is that, if I tell you the amount of the conditional legacy first, you will be very disappointed if you don't like the condition. So, if you will forgive me, I will just say that the amount is very substantial and then I shall give you a brief outline of the condition. Is that all right?'

Barbara's mouth had gone suddenly dry. It was all so very odd and she was not used to the unusual. Quite unable to reply in words, she nodded her agreement.

'The late Mr Thomas Lindley wanted you to have what he called "adventures".'

'Adventures?' Barbara repeated in surprise. 'Did you say "adventures"?'

'Well, er, yes.'
That was better. Barbara expected solicitors to say 'er'.
'What sort of adventures?'
This did not seem like real life at all.
'Travel, mainly.'
'Well, how can I possibly do that?' Barbara asked in disappointed tones. 'I only have three weeks holiday a year and,' she added disconsolately 'two of them have more or less to be spent at Frinton.'
'You would, I am afraid,' James continued, 'have to give up your present job.'
'Give up my job?'
Barbara's neat and orderly little world had crashed at her feet. Her whole life revolved around her job. How could she keep up her flat without her regular salary? How else could she even go to Frinton? And she did like Frinton really. How else could she live? She had known all along that this dream, like all her other dreams – some of them lovely, too – was nothing but a mirage in a desert of boredom.
James did not reply immediately. He realized that he had given Barbara a shock.
'It's a sort of gamble in a way,' he recommenced.
'Gamble!' Barbara echoed. She seemed to be doing little else but repeat what the solicitor had said. But she had been brought up to believe that gambling was even worse than – oh well, almost worse than anything. James Garton was an unusually sensitive young man and he saw at once that he had selected the wrong word for this particular young woman.
'I don't mean the race course,' he explained, smiling by way of apology.
'Perhaps "taking a risk" would be a better way of putting it.'
Barbara thought again of her dull but safe job and of her neat little flat.
'I'm not very good at taking risks,' she admitted.
'One of my old law lecturers,' said James, 'once said "The most dangerous thing you can do in this world is to get born in it".'
Barbara's long forgotten sense of humour popped up from the depths in which it had been buried for far too long.
'I did not, so far as I know, have to agree to that.'

James resisted the impulse to use the dry 'Quite so' that his senior partner would certainly have said. Instead, he just smiled and the atmosphere of the interview was transformed. There was more to this girl than there had seemed on the surface.

'Shall I tell you a little more, without prejudice, as we say?'

'Please do.'

James had really enjoyed drafting the will – normally a very uninteresting task – particularly after winning, from the somewhat reluctant Mr Lindley, permission to soften the condition a little. James knew this part of the will by heart.

'It amounts to a sort of treasure hunt,' he said.

'Tr ... ,' Barbara commenced, and smiled. She had, at long last, resisted the temptation to repeat everything the solicitor had said. Indeed, she suddenly began to feel a lot younger. She had very much enjoyed a treasure hunt that her school had organized after A levels. Perhaps it was the last thing that she had so thoroughly enjoyed; and eleven long years had passed by since then, only occasionally brightened by holidays and evenings out with Edna.

'The testator – your great-uncle – has left several clues for his treasure hunt. If you solve one and do what it says, you get another one, and so on. They will involve a great deal of travel, probably but not necessarily, alone, both in this island and abroad. None of it will be outside Europe, so don't worry about deserts and things like that. Your expenses will be paid on a generous scale and, if you succeed, you will receive fifty thousand pounds free of tax.'

'Fifty thousand pounds!' Barbara had reverted to her practice of repeating what was said to her.

'Yes.'

'But suppose that I can't solve the clues?'

James Garton was delighted by the question. Miss Lindley, as he then thought of her, had not said; 'But suppose that I can't do what the clue tells me to do?' On the other hand, she had foreseen the possibility that she might be accidentally frustrated by an insoluble clue. Barbara's actual question was one which he had raised himself at his second meeting with his late client.

'That is not an insuperable difficulty,' he replied. 'The

will gives me considerable discretion in that matter. Your great-uncle wanted you to have – I nearly said wants you to have, perhaps he does – what he called "adventures"; so, if you can convince me that you have made all reasonable efforts to solve a particular clue but without success, then I can give you clearer instructions. It is intended as a test of initiative and adventurousness, not of intellect.'

'Well that's something,' said Barbara, who did not consider herself to be an intellectual; but then neither was she particularly adventurous, or so she thought.

'But if that is so,' she continued, 'why bother with clues at all?'

'I own a model railway,' said James enigmatically.

Barbara, not surprisingly, looked very puzzled. Had the solicitor suddenly taken leave of his senses?

'Sorry. That was a very obscure remark. The point that I am trying to make is that most men never really grow up. Your late great-uncle's eyes sparkled with delight when he talked about his treasure hunt. I agree with you entirely that the introduction of clues is really illogical and more or less irrelevant. However, if I may put it like this, we are stuck with them.'

'Hm!' said Barbara. 'How long do I have to decide?'

'You have one month from now.'

'I see.'

They both sat in silence for a full minute. Like most people who have lived alone for some years, Barbara knew more about herself than an extrovert with a busy social life would have done. She did not waste that minute, she knew very well that once she started worrying about this, she would never jump. She found jumping very difficult; she always had. But suppose she committed herself now? Would not that be a good idea? If only she could persuade herself to do it. If she could – and it was a very big if – she would not be able to go back on it. Legally, no doubt she could, but according to her own, very personal code of honour, she could not. Perhaps that was why she never jumped.

Never?

'I'll agree now,' she said. And she was even more astonished than James was.

He rewarded her with his best smile.

'Your great-uncle would have been delighted to know that.'

'How do you know?'

'Your great-uncle was a dramatic old gentleman,' James explained, 'and although I saw him only three times, I feel that I knew him. Some people can have that effect on others; some can't.'

James paused.

'It is difficult to put into words what I feel,' he continued, 'but I do know that he really wanted you to succeed.'

'And did he,' Barbara remarked dryly, 'sound as though he expected me to?'

James hesitated. There was something about this young woman that compelled honesty.

'I don't think that he knew either way, but he certainly hoped so.'

'I shall try not to let him down,' Barbara promised, 'but I feel very puzzled about all this. Uncle Tom had a very gruff manner and I always got the impression that he didn't like me very much.'

'It would seem that you were wrong, said James. 'And now to business.'

He wrote out a cheque and handed it to her.

'Five hundred pounds,' she read with much astonishment.

'Yes, that's extra. It's unconditional. Mr Lindley said that he did not think that you would agree straight away, but he added, 'I am asking her to take considerable risks. I will take one too; it is only fair. Give her five hundred pounds extra if she agrees immediately'.'

Barbara suddenly felt very happy.

'What happens next?' she asked.

'Speaking as a lawyer,' said James, 'you must give a month's notice to your employer.'

'And then?'

'And then,' echoed James, 'I shall post the first clue to you in three weeks time, together with a cheque for expenses.'

'But won't the five hundred that you have just given me be enough?'

James smiled.

'That is not for expenses,' he said. 'When I said that it was extra, I meant just that. It's a gift.'

'It all sounds like a dream.'

'It does, I agree,' said James, 'but I am afraid that, unlike a dream, it won't just happen. You will have to make it happen, won't you?'

3

Barbara went back to her little flat, walking on air. She had often heard the phrase but never actually experienced it for herself. She seemed to be using no energy at all; it felt almost like floating. This was the most amazing thing that had ever happened to her, perhaps the only really amazing thing.

She went inside and made herself a real treat supper: soup and curry and rice. In the old days, she would not have bothered; how odd. But is was not really so very odd. What had just happened to her was so vivid that she was interested in everything, even in so ordinary a thing as her lonely supper.

Then, quite suddenly, a reaction set in. She must have been mad to agree without proper thought; most unlike her. She looked at all her nice things: the book case full of her favourite books, the lovely patterned carpet, picked up as a bargain at a sale, the grandmother clock that she had saved up for with such determination and enthusiasm and the carefully chosen pictures on the wall – not expensive ones, of course, but favourites that she had so pleasurably chosen over the years. Two hours ago, she had had a secure job – not a very interesting one it is true, but safe, a cosy flat and one very reliable friend. She somehow felt that she was deserting her flat, which, she admitted to herself, was nonsense, because it would still be there as a welcome haven every time that she returned from her travels. As for Edna, she might well think that Barbara was deserting her. Barbara had nearly always been at home when she rang or called; now perhaps next time, Barbara might be in Timbuctu. No, she must not exaggerate. Mr Garton had said, ' . . . in this country or in Europe.' It did not occur to Barbara at all that her decision was not irrevocable. To her it was; she had never blown hot and cold and she did not intend to start now. She had agreed to take on this extraordinary adventure and, although, as she suspected, James would have confirmed that she could return the cheque uncashed and that would be the end of the matter, such an idea was never allowed to take hold. She was normally, although not on this particular occasion, desperately slow in deciding anything but, once decided, that was that. The same rule applied to this rare, rapid decision. Barbara was a great one for sticking to the rules. It suddenly dawned on her that she was, in a way, looking forward, although with some trepidation, to the adventures, whatever they might turn out to be, more than she was to the possibility of receiving a huge legacy. There were two reasons for this. One was that, as her great-uncle had suspected there was, deep inside her, a feeling that she was missing out on life. The other was that money, even if she were to win it by her own efforts, was not something that she had ever given much thought to. Money was necessary but, in itself, uninteresting. Suddenly, for the second time that day, she was amused at herself and her own reactions. She realized that she was going over in her mind a mixed recollection of two clichés, and she did not really like clichés. She had burnt her boats and she had not yet crossed the Rubicon, although she was now completely committed to do so. But how on earth was she to do so without a boat? As she was to find several times in the near future, her sense of humour, for so long suppressed, was one of her principal allies.

Feeling somewhat cheered but not yet anything like able to adjust to this incredible change in her fortunes, she watched a television programme, which cheered her still more. It was something of an adventure story itself, and for the first time ever, Barbara felt, when it was over, 'I'm not just an armchair adventurer' – funny that she could not say 'adventuress' but languages are funny things – 'I'm a real one, or at least I very soon shall be.'

Barbara always read in bed and she was in the middle of Nevil Shute's *No Highway*. That night, she read much longer than usual before she felt sleepy. After turning out the light, she began to think that there was perhaps some similarity between her and Mr Honey in the novel – not much but a little. They were both dragged into adventures that they had not sought. There, no doubt, the comparison ended, but wasn't it odd that twice in one evening she had begun to identify herself with fictional heroes? Still thinking about this, Barbara fell asleep.

The next morning, she was quite convinced that she had had a strange dream; and she felt very let down. Indeed, she was so nearly sure that the whole thing was a figment of her imagination that she was not fully convinced otherwise until she had found the cheque. It was real after all. She could not quite make up her mind whether to say 'Hurray' or 'Oh dear.'

Anyway, the die was now cast; and she set off for the office with curiously mixed feelings. Was she to rejoice that she had escaped from prison or to be frightened of the future? At the first convenient opportunity, she went in to see her supervisor and handed in her written resignation. Lilian, the supervisor, looked very surprised.

'I thought you were a fixture here, Barbara, like me.'

'I thought so too.'

'I don't want to be inquisitive,' said Lilian, 'so don't tell me if you don't want to, but what's the new job?'

'There isn't one, I'm afraid.'

Lilian was speechless.

'I've been left some money in a will,' Barbara explained.

She had decided that part of the truth would be best and she continued,

'I'm going on a long holiday first.'

'Lucky you.'

Barbara returned to her desk, picked up her notebook and started work again. No job, however dull and uninteresting, can be depressing if you are doing it for a month. The same thought had often occurred to her when sixth formers and others had come to do temporary jobs during their long summer holidays. 'No wonder they are so cheerful,' she had thought. 'They are not bound to do it for ever.' Well, now she wasn't either.

Several of the girls tried to tie her down to details, but Barbara still did not know whether she was going to succeed, so she parried their questions with replies like,

'Well, I've inherited enough for a good long holiday and to keep me going afterwards for a bit.'

'While you look for a new job?'

'I expect so,' she replied, and she could not make up her mind whether she was being polite or pessimistic.

Most of the other girls were not particularly surprised that Barbara was being so uninformative. She had always been very reserved and, as some of them thought, stand-offish. No, they were not surprised by that. What did surprise them was that she was actually leaving at all. Indeed, Barbara overheard one of them remark to a friend,

'The worm has turned at last. I didn't think the poor dear would ever leave.'

Barbara felt very hurt by that comment, although she decided that it was something that the girl had not said 'the poor OLD dear.' The girl was seventeen and Barbara twenty-nine, so she might even have said that. 'Old people' seemed to include anybody over twenty-five these days! Then Barbara smiled to herself. 'They would be very surprised if they really knew what had happened,' she thought. She realized that she would have no real regrets at all about leaving the office. She had not made any real friends there. It was true that she liked Anne, a girl a little younger than she, but the friendship did not extend beyond having lunch together occasionally. At least, Anne was more or less on the same wavelength. Barbara would miss her when she left.

She got up in answer to a bell. Uncle Tom had been right, she was not a real secretary; she frequently changed her boss within the firm. Her boss that week did not seem irritating any more. With the background of her new freedom, Barbara discovered that she could now persuade him to allow a very neat correction instead of his insisting on a complete re-type of a long letter. 'To him that hath shall be given.' Barbara had no sympathy with 'Women's Lib' and felt no temptation to alter the second word to 'her'.

About a week before her notice expired, and, rather considerately on a Friday, Barbara duly received the promised letter from James.

Dear Miss Lindley,

I now have pleasure in enclosing the first of the clues in the treasure hunt as defined by the will of the late Mr Lindley. I

sincerely hope that you can solve it. If not, please let me know and we shall see what can be done about it.

The clue is: 'The late Herr Richard Schirrmann invented, or perhaps originated would be a better word, something. Use five of them in this island.' I wish you the best of luck with this. I think that you will enjoy it. When you have solved the conundrum (with or without my help) I must, I regret, ask you to bring me some evidence. That sounds very discourteous, but it is legally necessary.

Yours sincerely,

James Garton.

Who on earth was Herr Richard Schirrmann and what did he invent or originate? In any case, how could anyone invent or even originate a place? The words 'in this island' seemed to suggest a place. The letter arrived just before she set out for the office, and it worried her a little. How ever was she to set about solving the clue? But Barbara was very self-disciplined and she more or less succeeded in putting the problem out of her mind for the rest of the day.

On the following morning, she got up fairly early and, as soon as the public library was open, she set out eagerly to investigate. She tried *Who's Who* and *Who Was Who* without success. That was disappointing. She did not know what to do next. Obviously, she would have to make several reasonable tries before being entitled to ask the solicitor for help. In any case, she very much wanted to find the answer herself, if at all possible. She went to the girl at the desk and put the problem to her.

'We have some indexes of obituaries,' she said.

To Barbara's pleasure, the name appeared there.

'We don't have the obituary here,' the librarian said, 'but for a small fee, I can get a micro-film of it for you before next Saturday.'

Barbara had to be content with that. It seemed something of an anticlimax. Feeling a little deflated, but being fairly sure that the clue would be solved a week later, Barbara went home.

After what seemed like a month, the next Saturday dawned.

Once again, Barbara set off. The micro-film had arrived as promised, and feeling rather like an explorer, Barbara duly put it into the machine and read it. Herr Richard Schirrmann was, it appeared, the founder of the Youth Hostel Movement. She had heard of such hostels, of course, but her ideas on the subject were very vague indeed. What exactly were they and how was she to set about using five of them? A quick search in a telephone directory gave her an address, and off she set for the Youth Hostels place in London. A real step in the right direction at last.

Unfortunately, as it seemed to her, it was a young man who dealt with her there and in view of her abysmal ignorance she felt very embarrassed. She felt that a woman might have been more sympathetic. Men always seemed to know everything and to be surprised if you didn't too.

'If I want to use Youth Hostels,' she asked, 'how do I go about it?'

'You become a member of the YHA – sorry Youth Hostels Association,' he replied pleasantly. 'I'll give you a form and you can enrol on the spot.'

If Barbara had expected him to say, 'Don't you know what to do? You must be very silly,' she would have been wrong, but something of the sort, although perhaps not so discourteously expressed, had occurred to her as a possibility. She duly completed the form, paid a fee and received a membership card and handbook.

'Please read the rules in the handbook,' she was advised. 'They will make everything clear, I think.'

The building also contained a very large shop with a bewildering variety of outdoor clothing, and she decided to wander around looking at it. She did not really know what to buy and was pleased that she could browse round without being pestered with questions. After a while, she went up to a woman assistant of about her own age.

'I wonder if you could help me,' she said. 'I have just become a member and I don't quite know what I should buy.'

The girl looked a little baffled by so general a question and asked, 'To wear, you mean?'

As the shop had seemed to contain nothing but clothing, Barbara thought the question somewhat odd but felt no temptation to reply, 'I was really looking for a steam-roller,' or make any other jocular but probably irritating comment.

'Well, yes,' she said, 'and anything else I ought to have.' (What else was there in this shop?)

'Walking or cycling?'

'Walking.'

The girl proved most helpful; and Barbara felt like a Christmas tree, laden with clothes, including boots and a thin sheet sleeping bag. The assistant gave her some advice about the boots.

'For heaven's sake, use them a bit, before setting off on a tour,' she said. 'Why not wander about in them at dead of night if you feel awkward about it?'

'Well, thank you,' said Barbara, 'but it might be a bit dangerous to saunter about in the middle of the night where I live. I've got what I need to wear, what about maps and things? Where do I get them?'

'We have a map and book department. Where are you thinking of going?'

'The Lake District.'

'Right. Well, if I were you, I would get the special Ordnance Survey maps of the area. I certainly recommend the two and a halfs.'

'Please,' Barbara said, 'what are two and a halfs?'

'Sorry,' the girl said, 'they are maps on a scale of about two and a half inches to the mile. The special maps are in that scale. They show much more detail than the standard maps.'

'I'll do that,' Barbara agreed. 'What else ought I to have?'

'Two things, I think. A good compass is essential, and I'd take a small first-aid kit with you if I were you.'

'Blisters and things?'

'Yes – or little cuts and bruises.'

'You do make it sound fun,' said Barbara and added, more seriously, 'I've sometimes thought that a blister might ruin the whole thing. What should I do about them?'

The girl looked round in a conspiratorial way.

'Well; if it is just a water-blister – and most of them are, I would prick it, but some people say that it is dangerous to do that. What I do myself is sterilize a needle by putting it in the flame of a match. I have done it dozens of times and I am still walking around. Trying to walk on a bad blister is very painful, I can tell you. Put a bit of plaster on as well, of course.'

'Thank you very much,' said Barbara. 'You have been most helpful to me. And thank you too for not making me feel like an idiot. I have done a bit of gentle walking near London, but I expect that most of your customers know what they are talking about?'

'It is nice to have someone who actually listened to my advice,' said the girl, 'and don't forget to take the sleeping-bag, they are compulsory at hostels and it is dear to hire one every night.'

Barbara later emerged from the shop and started for home. As she had bought a large framed rucksack, all her purchases were safely stowed away.

'Ah well,' she thought as she walked along The Strand, 'I don't suppose that this is the oddest thing I shall have to do.' But she did feel a bit out of place dressed in ordinary town clothing and wearing a rucksack.

That evening, but before it was dark, she decided to follow the advice she had been given and put on her new boots for a short local walk. London being London, nobody gave her a second glance. If some idiot wanted to parade around in boots, she could get on with it for all Londoners cared. Perhaps that was what made London such a lonely place sometimes.

Back home again, she read conscientiously through the rules in the little handbook so that she would know exactly what to do and what to expect.

When the last office day came – and, until so recently she had assumed that she would be sixty years old when that happened! – she felt very odd indeed. She was quite pleased with the little farewell ceremony and presentation, a new watch, the feminine equivalent of the traditional retirement present of a clock. What pleased her even more than the little present and the speech, however, was that not only then but throughout her last month at work, almost everybody seemed much more friendly to her than they had ever been before. She was not really able to work out why.

After the ceremony, Lilian invited Barbara to her little sanctum for a personal farewell.

'Barbara,' she said. 'You are a different person.'

'Oh?'

'I don't know how to say it, actually,' said Lilian. 'The best way I can put it is that you look five years younger.'

'Thank you.'

(Perhaps that was what had made everyone seem friendlier?)

'I wish some rich uncle, or whoever, would leave me a fortune.'

Barbara almost wondered whether someone had been looking at the will, but they would not have known where to start looking.

'Who said anything about a fortune?'

'Well, perhaps not a fortune exactly,' Lilian replied, 'but enough to get out of here would do me very well,' she said, grimly.

The last to say 'Good-bye' was Anne.

'All the luck in the world, Barbara.'

She said it very cheerfully, but she looked a little sad.

4

Barbara was looking forward to telling Edna all about this sudden change in her fortunes; happiness really needs to be shared. Barbara invited her friend to her flat for a little dinner. Edna was, as Barbara had expected, suitably surprised by the news but she did her best to hide a feeling of – well, not exactly envy but a sensation of being left behind. She was three years older than Barbara and very fond of her.

'I'm very, very glad for you, Barbara,' she said 'but it is the parting of the ways, isn't it?'

'I don't see why it should be,' said Barbara, surprised. 'I'm keeping on the flat and I don't suppose that I shall be away for more than two or three weeks at a time. I'm not going to the Antipodes, you know.'

'I did not quite mean that,' Edna replied. 'It is just that, somehow, I had thought that I would always have you, whoever and whatever else disappeared.'

'But you still have.'

'Not quite as it was.'

'Who knows?'

'I do,' said Edna sadly.

Strangely enough, it was Edna who realized, long before her friend did, that Barbara had been released. The word, which was in her mind although she did not say it aloud, seemed an odd one, but it was, she thought, exactly right. Barbara had been let off the lead. Edna was very fond of dogs and sorry that she could not keep one. Mind you, she thought, being let off the lead can be dangerous too, and she admitted reluctantly to herself that in all probability she would not have accepted the challenge.

'Don't ever forget me, will you, Barbara?'

'Of course not,' said Barbara. 'You are worrying about

nothing, Edna. In any case, I am sure that I don't deserve all this. You will turn my head if you are not careful.'

The very next day, Barbara set off for Clapham South tube station *en route* for Euston. She felt very odd in her strange new clothes – boots, breeches and an anorak, but she was a great believer in following the advice of an expert. So if this was the recommended gear for a walking tour, that was what she would wear. She was rather surprised that it made her feel quite energetic already. There was a lot to be said for dressing the part. She arrived at Euston very early for her train and bought a monthly return to Penrith. Then she had a cup of coffee and got a novel to read on the journey.

Like many southerners, Barbara was convinced that the North began at Watford, and she thoroughly enjoyed looking out of the window, even when the train wound its way through industrial areas. Nobody spoke to her on the train and she was not the sort of person to strike up a conversation with a complete stranger; she rather wished that she was. Nevertheless, she found it an exhilarating journey as the train sped North. It seemed lovely to her that nobody could get at her on the train; it was like being on a very pleasant island. Why anybody should spoil the peace by carrying a radio-telephone wherever they went was a mystery to her.

It seemed very strange indeed setting off all by herself from Penrith. The air was pure and fresh, and it gave her a lovely feeling of freedom and energy. She was not worried about the walking itself; she had had a number of day rambles with her father when she was a child, and even Edna had occasionally come with her for some pretty energetic walks in Surrey and Kent. But this was quite different and the countryside much less gentle.

On the first day, she did not have time to cover a great distance, but she thoroughly enjoyed the eight hilly miles to her first hostel. The girl in the YHA shop had known what she was talking about; the strange get-up was really very comfortable now that she was getting used to it, and she found herself positively striding along. She dropped down from the hills towards the hostel with some trepidation. As she approached the hostel, she began to see more clearly a farmhouse – or so it appeared to be – in a little lane. The farmhouse had been turned into a hostel.

Barbara had a horror of looking foolish and she became more and more conscious of her ignorance of hostelling as she approached the building. However, typical of Barbara, she had read up the subject at great length before setting out. So much of her knowledge of life had until then been learnt from books that it had been a refreshingly new experience for her to read about something that she was actually going to do. Now was the end of theory and the beginning of practice. Unfortunately, she was not at all the sort of person who could bluff her way through life – how lucky, she thought, such people were. She decided to be completely honest.

The warden in charge of the hostel did not look as though he would bite and so she said,

'Good evening. I have never used a hostel before.'

'Thanks for telling me,' the warden replied. 'I've always been sorry that I once made a girl cry, because I ticked her off for doing something that an experienced hosteller would never had done. It turned out to be her first hostel too, but she looked and sounded so used to it.'

'Well, I don't suppose I do.' Barbara smiled. 'In any case, I have admitted that I am not. I hope I haven't done anything dreadful already.'

The warden looked a little apologetic.

'Well, actually,' he said, 'there is something you haven't done.'

'Oh dear. Good heavens, I forgot. I am supposed to have taken my boots off in the entrance.'

'Never mind. It did not matter much in this dry weather.'

'Sorry, anyway. I'll do it now.'

'I have put you in Dormitory Two. You know about doing a job in hostels do you?'

'Yes.'

'Good. Will you please sweep your own dormitory tomorrow morning. There,' said the warden, pointing, 'is the broom cupboard.'

'Certainly.'

With the preliminaries over, Barbara made her way up to the dormitory, which turned out to contain six double-bunks. She had achieved her first aim, to get there first – not because she wanted to grab the best bed but because she felt that it would be easier to greet the others in ones and twos rather than to arrive in the middle of things. Barbara fully realized that she was still being much too cautious, but she was rather proud of tackling this thing at all and readily forgave herself for retaining some of her old characteristics. Much as she would have liked to do so, she could not suddenly become a quite different girl. She found the wash-room fairly primitive but adequate, with some surprisingly hot water, which was most welcome. Then, she made her bed. She had, rather pathetically perhaps, practised doing so with the special sleeping-bag at home.

There was over an hour and a half before supper, so she decided to explore the hostel. It was very well signposted, so, after her brief tour of inspection, she settled down to read in the common room. She was still very keyed up and was very glad that she had bought such a light novel at Euston; she could not possibly have concentrated on a serious book. She was glad when, about twenty minutes later, two others, fortunately girls, came in.

'Good evening,' she said politely.

'Hello,' they said.

Barbara docketed in her mind, for future use, that 'Good evening' was too formal.

There was a short silence.

'Wocking?' said one of the newcomers.

'No,' said Barbara, somewhat taken aback, 'I'm not working, I'm on holiday.'

'I said "wocking" not "worrking".'

'Oh, I'm sorry.'

'Not to worry. They tell me that my Glasgow accent is unintelligible.'

'I've not been to Scotland,' Barbara admitted.

'Well, you should. It's a fine country.'

Barbara was delighted that the first person she had talked to in the hostel seemed so friendly and had not been at all offended that she had not begun to make sense of her opening remark. Gradually, the common room began to fill up and Barbara found that she felt at home surprisingly quickly. She was not normally particularly good at talking to strangers, but here, with very rare exceptions, everybody seemed to be very happy and good at communicating this to other people.

The supper turned out to be simple, but very good and ample. To Barbara's pleasure and surprise, the meal began with soup. Indeed the supper was more than Barbara wanted on that first day. The novelty of her surroundings had taken away most of her appetite. At the meal she was sitting next to two eighteen year old boys who were with their own group of friends, but they did not ignore Barbara but brought her into the conversation quite as though she were one of themselves. It was an unusual and delightful experience for her. For so many years, she had felt that she could not talk to people in this casual way. She began to feel very grateful to Uncle Tom. This was all very odd, but it was much, much better than being all by herself in the flat, eating beans on toast, not that there was anything wrong in eating beans on toast. The only difficulty so far was the technical language and the amazing variety of dialects. What on earth was a self-cooker? It sounded like a cannibal; and then it dawned on her: of course, if you did not have the warden's meals, you cooked your own in the members' kitchen. Indeed, in some hostels there were no warden's meals, but Barbara had prepared enough meals for herself at home that she had no wish to try one of those.

Afterwards, there was a sing-song, and although she took no real part in it, she enjoyed listening, and the feeling of togetherness that it gave. Her great enjoyment of the new experience after the energetic walk saw to it that within a few minutes of climbing into her bunk she was sound asleep.

When Barbara awoke in the morning, she could not at first realize where she was. As she was in an upper bunk, the ceiling seemed surprisingly low. As she came fully to her senses, she realized exactly where she was and she got up – or, strictly, down, and it seemed an awfully long way to the floor. After that it seemed very odd washing and dressing 'in public', an experience entirely new to her. After a much larger breakfast than she was used to, she duly swept the dormitory and, to her surprise, very much enjoyed it; it seemed an odd thing to enjoy. Not only did it make her feel a real hosteller but it was also very pleasing to see how the others all went to a lot of trouble to move their things out of her way, unasked. There was a lovely feeling of co-operation, something sadly lacking in Barbara's old life.

The weather was lovely, bright and fine. As she had booked two nights at the same hostel, she had packed, inside the large rucksack, a small haversack, just to contain her packed lunch, a map and a mack. It felt very light after the big rucksack. Once again, she had the feeling of weightlessness. Why bother to go into space? As she left the hostel, she felt freer than she had ever done in her life. She would have been surprised, had she known, that an elderly man in a bus, which happened to be passing at the moment, wondered why she looked so happy. The scenery was easily the most magnificent that she had ever seen, with mountains and tarns and distant views of larger lakes sparkling in the distance. Everything looked green, blue or a shade of grey – such clear-cut colours and such breath taking views. For the first time on this holiday, as she was now beginning to think of it, Barbara realized that the people in her old office were actually hard at work, typing away like mad, and here she was striding along in this glorious countryside. It did not seem fair. At a corner in the path she came unexpectedly upon a tiny waterfall gushing down the mountainside, with the spray glinting in the sun. In the rushing water were all the colours of the rainbow – violet, indigo, blue, green, yellow, orange and red. In the afternoon, she dropped down to a little village and found a cottage which advertised teas. She tried some rum butter, a speciality in that part of the world. Much refreshed, she walked back to the hostel.

She was beginning already to feel much more experienced and, notwithstanding the tea, she was much hungrier for the evening meal than she had been on the first day. Hardly surprising! The hostel was much more crowded than it had been on the first night and she did not know the girl who was sleeping on the lower bunk. As Barbara got ready to climb into the upper one, the girl below, noticing Barbara's somewhat prim nightie, said,

'Slumming are you?'

It was the first unkind remark that had been made to Barbara since it had all begun. She had been feeling so proud of mixing so quickly and happily with everybody else that the comment took her completely by surprise and she was quite unable to think of a suitable reply. To her extreme embarrassment, she looked, she knew, very hurt and, which was even worse, she made a tiny sob.

The girl below was contrite.

'Sorry, love,' she said. 'You from the South?'

'Yes.'

'Well, you'll have to get used to us Northerners, won't you? But I am sorry, really.'

Much comforted by the apology and by the word 'Love', although it probably did not mean very much, Barbara settled into her cosy bunk. As she gradually fell asleep, she began to realize what, perhaps, Uncle Tom had had in mind. Mixing with other people meant exposing yourself to them. There had been nobody in her flat to comment on what she chose to wear in bed.

The next day she was moving on to another hostel and she again shouldered her large rucksack. She collected her membership card and was interested to see that the Warden had stamped it with a little picture of the hostel. She later discovered that each hostel had a distinctive rubber stamp. What attractive souvenirs they made.

Barbara had decided to be really energetic that day and to walk fourteen miles over some quite tough country. She thoroughly enjoyed it, but is was a quite different kind of pleasure from the day before. She glanced at her watch from time to time – the new watch that had been given to her as a parting present – to check how she was doing. It was typical of her that she had made a detailed timetable the night before. It worked, so she was tired but very happy when she arrived at the next hostel. This one was quite different from the first. It had actually been built as a hostel, was not a converted farmhouse, and was very impressive to look at. It was, however, much less homely.

That evening, for the first time in that holiday, she had a really long conversation with another girl who was also walking alone. Her name was Lynne, and she was a young schoolmistress from Manchester, enjoying a week's half-term break. It turned out that she was going on to the same hostel that Barbara was making for the next day.

'Are you staying there just for one night?' Lynne asked.

'No,' Barbara replied. 'Two.'

'Would you like it if we walked together tomorrow?'

'If you would,' Barbara replied.

'Yes, very much.'

'Why did you ask me first if I was staying one night or two?'

'You would ask that, wouldn't you?' Lynne countered, smiling. 'Well, if you must know, I'm something of a loner, but I would really enjoy your company for one day.'

'And if I had been staying there for only one night, you might have been stuck with me?' Barbara asked quite pleasantly.

'Well, yes, if you insist, but I would really enjoy it if you come with me tomorrow.'

With that rather second-class compliment, Barbara had to be content. In any case, it quite suited her; she was something of a loner herself. But she had been a bit the odd one out so far, and it would be very nice to have a day with her new friend.

By the following morning, the weather had changed, and for most of the day Barbara and Lynne were walking in thin mountain rain. In its way, it was invigorating and it gave them the feeling of being the only living creatures in the world. It was a particularly fortunate day to have a companion. It would have felt really eerie walking alone. There were absolutely no views, and on the infrequent occasions that they passed other walkers, it felt rather like being in an open-air cinema. Figures suddenly appeared out of the mist, as though on a screen, and as suddenly vanished again.

Barbara learnt a lot about walking and hostelling by talking to Lynne most of the day. After all, there was nothing to see.

'Do you mind doing the little jobs they ask you to do in the hostels?' Lynne asked.

'Why ever should I?'

'Well, I agree; but some people seem to take a dim view of it.'

'I can't think why.'

'I'll tell you a story – a true one,' Lynne began. 'A new Regional Secretary had been appointed. Secretaries are office people and some of them are not actually hostellers themselves. Well, this one – John his name was – had to spend a night at a hostel after a conference there. The next morning the warden went up to the Chairman of the Region – he always is a hosteller – and said, "Jack, sweep the top corridor, will you?" John, the new Secretary expected the heavens to open and lightning to strike; more seriously, he wondered, as he told me later, whether the warden would be sacked on the spot. Much to his surprise, the Chairman said, "OK, I'll do it straight away".'

'There is nothing undignified in honest work,' said Barbara but, as she said it, she wished that it did not sound quite so trite – a pity because she really meant what she said; she usually did.

During one of their silent periods, Barbara began to muse about the strange experiences she was having. Here she was, walking in a thick mist, with a girl whom she had known for less than twenty-four hours. She quickly realized that she had been living much too sheltered a life for far too long. No wonder people looked at her oddly sometimes. She certainly did not wish to be a modern bachelor girl with seemingly endless boyfriends and parties. But, if she was a few years out-of-date, she was certainly catching up now as fast as she could, although, as yet, no parties or boyfriends. She was very pleased with her progress so far. There would be slip-ups, she realized, like the remark about her nightie, but she was quite determined to ride them. Walking through a wet mist seemed remarkably conducive to thought. After some minutes silence, Lynne said,

'Nearly all the holidays I can spare I come to the Lakes. I know them like the back of my hand.'

It reminded Barbara of Edna and her insistence on Frinton-on-Sea. With a slight feeling of disloyalty to her friend, Barbara thought that the Lakes were a better choice.

'The Lake District is quite new to me,' Barbara said, 'but I have seen so little north of London that I may try another area next time.'

'You won't like it so much,' said Lynne with confidence.

They trudged on and found a corner between two stone walls for their sandwiches. It seemed quite a retreat in the thick mist, surprisingly cosy and intimate.

Early in the evening, the hostel suddenly loomed up out of the gloom. Although that was the only occasion on this trip that Barbara had a companion during the day, she found interesting people to talk to every evening in each of the hostels.

One night, a group of girls on an 'Outward Bound' course were staying at the same hostel as Barbara. They had obviously had a very energetic day and they were contentedly reading or writing in the common room, when their leader, hardly raising her voice above a conversational level, said,

'Time for bed, girls.'

They were all somewhere between sixteen and eighteen years old, but they all immediately and cheerfully closed their books or stopped writing and trooped happily off to the dormitories. When they had all gone, Barbara went up to the leader and said,

'I am very impressed.'

'What with?'

'The way they all went off so quickly when you told them to.'

'Of course they did.'

Barbara was moving away, feeling rebuffed – but her remark had been intended as a sincere compliment, not as interference – when the leader called her back.

'I think I can explain if it really interests you,' she said. 'You see they are all doing quite tough and difficult things. I thought one of them was going to fall off a rock today. They have impressed me, and themselves, by doing what they have been doing all day. They don't have to show off by being disobedient to what my husband – he is an army officer – would call a "lawful command". Satisfied?'

'Yes, thank you,' Barbara replied. 'I see. Yes, they would feel confident, I suppose, and they don't have to prove it in the wrong way. Is that what you mean?'

'Exactly. Good night.'

Barbara felt that she too had been dismissed, surprised that she had subconsciously obeyed what was certainly not intended to be a 'lawful command' but it did so sound like one.

All things, however odd, come to an end, not that hostelling any longer seemed odd to Barbara. Indeed, she was really sorry when the time came for her to board the train at Oxenholme. She had had the most worthwhile holiday that she had ever had, and now it was over.

As Churchill had said: 'the end of the beginning'. Who

knows what her great-uncle had in store for her?

As she sat reading in the train and looking from time to time out of the window at the varied scenery as it flashed past, she felt very rested and happy and, in the pleasantest possible way, superior to most other people in the train, who had quite obviously not been walking or, indeed, much in the open air at all. Most of them did not even bother to raise their eyes to look at the changing views. Some of her fellow passengers seemed to be travelling on business of some kind, and Barbara noticed, more clearly than ever before, how nervy and impatient some of them were. Four or five miles short of Euston, they fussily gathered their papers together, put them in a shiny brief-case and started walking to the front of the train. Was two minutes so very important to them? Barbara stayed put and wondered about it. She had not had to hurry for a whole glorious week and she was not about to start now.

5

Barbara got back to her little flat feeling very happy. The first hurdle had been surmounted and she had really enjoyed doing it. She rang James Garton the very next morning and went to see him in the afternoon. He positively encouraged her to give a detailed and vivid account of her travels – a pleasant change for him from conveyancing – and was rather amused at having to inspect her membership card.

'I'm used to examining deeds,' he said, 'but I have never had to consider one of these things before. They were not part of my law course. That is all very satisfactory,' he added, returning the card to Barbara.

'Now, the next clue is, in my opinion, well-nigh impossible to solve; it certainly baffled me – but don't worry – I shall exercise my discretion to give you a much more intelligible hint if you have to give this one up by the end of the week.'

'I thought you said that you were baffled yourself?'

'Well, I should have emphasized that I *was* baffled,' James admitted, 'but your great-uncle left me a detailed explanation. You asked that question very quickly. You should train for the Bar.'

He handed Barbara a piece of paper on which was written the one word: 'Merlota.'

'It certainly conveys nothing at all to me at the moment,' Barbara admitted.

She left Lincoln's Inn and went straight to the reference library. She thought at first that it might be a place in Italy or Spain. However, she drew a complete blank with the index to an enormous atlas of the world. She did not know what to try after that and went back to her desk to think for a while. After a few minutes, it dawned on her that part of Uncle Tom's plan was, fairly obviously, to make her move around – not just among places but among people too, perhaps especially among people. She was rather amused by the idea that she should write a huge placard reading

MERLOTA
What does it mean?

Prize £5.00

and set it up in The Strand, or walk up and down with it like a sandwich-board man. But what actually to do?

She had arranged an evening out with Edna. She took the opportunity of asking her, but with absolutely no result. Edna was equally baffled but she was not one of those irritating people who make wild and completely useless guesses.

Barbara was pretty sure that it was not French or German but suspected that it was some foreign language or other. Dictionaries in a variety of strange tongues produced no answer to the problem. She had, alas, surprisingly few friends whom she could ask, and she could hardly, in real life, stop perfect strangers in the street, with or without the aid of a placard and with or without the offer of a reward. She sat and pondered. A bright idea – at least she hoped it was – suddenly occurred to her. Lying on the mat when she had returned from the Lake District, was an invitation to a candlelight supper organized by the Old Girls' Association of her School. Normally she had, with some slight reluctance, ignored these annual invitations but, here and now, it seemed a good opportunity of seeing a large number of people of a type who might well be able to solve an intellectual puzzle, so she sent an acceptance.

As she had not been to one of these reunions for years, she felt a little shy when she arrived. She need not have worried. She was delighted to find that several of her old friends were there and seemed, to her surprise, very glad to see her. Nevertheless, it was a little deflating in a way because so many of them seemed to have married and even to have started a family.

Although Barbara was not exactly a teetotaller, she drank very little, but, as the evening wore on, and she discovered that it was impossible for her to say in a nonchalant way, 'By the way do you know what "Merlota" means?' she came to the conclusion that a couple of glasses of white wine might make it easier. After trying the experiment, she found herself talking to a girl with the strange name, as it seemed to Barbara, of Nest; she pronounced it something like 'Naist'. Barbara had always thought that it was a beautiful name and had discovered at School that she was Welsh. Nest was, by now, a translator in the office of a foreign bank in London and was, not surprisingly, a competent linguist. She was telling Barbara at some length about her job. It was a rare treat to listen to an enthusiast about anything; Barbara would certainly not have been able to sound so keen about her old job. In a rare pause, Barbara summoned up the courage to ask,

'Do you happen to know what Merlota means?'

She felt very silly; there was no real context.

'Whatever do you want to know that for?'

Barbara was completely taken aback. Being normally quite remarkably non-conspiratorial, she was not in the habit of preparing, in advance, answers to predictable questions.

'I – er – met it in something I was reading.'

Well, that was true, wasn't it?

'It means pony-trekking,' Nest replied. 'At least that is what it usually means, but I suppose that it is any kind of riding really.'

'Thank you,' said Barbara. 'What language is it?'

'Welsh, of course.'

She sounded nearly as staccato as the Outward Bound leader had been.

'You will have to take my word for what it means, I'm afraid,' Nest added in a much less didactic tone.

That seemed a surprising remark.

'What do you mean?'

'It's a fairly modern word actually. You probably won't find it in your dictionary, unless it is a recent publication. It comes from a word that you will find in any dictionary though, "merlyn" which means "pony".'

Why on earth should Nest assume that Barbara had a Welsh dictionary and that it should be out-of-date? Barbara was amused to imagine her little flat crammed with dictionaries of endless unlikely languages – not that Nest would have considered that Welsh was in the least unlikely.

'I'm very glad that you knew the word,' said Barbara.

'Why ever should you be so glad?' said Nest. 'You sound as though I had just given you a hundred pounds.'

That was so close to the truth that Barbara hesitated before replying.

'Well – er,' she said, after some fast thought – and she was not used to thinking rapidly, 'It's a sort of adventure story that I am reading and I couldn't quite understand the story without knowing that word.' Barbara was not a good liar, even though there was some truth in what she had said, and she felt herself blushing. Nest seemed not to notice it.

'Funny sort of story,' was all she said.

It was indeed.

The next day, Barbara again went to the reference library, but this time she knew exactly what she was looking for. She found a list of recommended trekking holidays, chose one in Wales, because she assumed that that was what her great-uncle had intended, went home and promptly sent off a booking for a week. It occurred to her afterwards that she had made no attempt to check the accuracy of Nest's translation, but Barbara did not go about checking up on things. In any case, Nest had clearly known what she was talking about.

Barbara thoroughly enjoyed the next few days with nothing special to do except to read up all she could about riding. She began to feel somewhat nervous about it, but comforted herself with the fact that the advertisement had clearly stated that absolute beginners were welcome. One thing that really did surprise Barbara at that time was how well she felt. She had, of course, had a very energetic walking-tour in the Lake District, so it was not particularly surprising that she should feel healthy. But there was more to it than that; she was enjoying the whole amazing adventure, even when, as now she was a little frightened of taking the next step. Indeed, she was quite pleasantly surprised at herself. A few days later, she set off for South Wales. She had never been there before and, like most English people, she supposed that it consisted of coal-mines and factories. How wrong she was.

The riding school was not residential but the brochure had recommended several addresses for bed, breakfast and evening meal. She had selected a small guest-house and was delighted when she saw it. It was a lovely old house with exposed beams, not only in the dining-room but in her own surprisingly spacious bedroom.

She felt very nervous the next morning. She had felt very odd and conspicuous the first time that she had donned proper walking clothes, but it seemed even odder to wear a hard hat as well. Fortunately, it was soon clear that there were other novices and that they were to be introduced to riding quite gradually. Thank heaven for that. She was very relieved that they were not to be thrown in at the deep end. On the first morning, they simply sat on horse-back and walked slowly around like small children being taught to ride. Even that felt very odd. Barbara had never realized before how far from the ground it would feel. What a difference height made. Perhaps that was what made riders look like superior beings – just that they were taller, that is all. Barbara was beginning to feel a little more confident on the back of a pony when the tutor cunningly made them go downhill for the first time. Barbara had become so used to seeing the friendly head of her pony in front of her that when it suddenly disappeared she felt quite lost without its friendly protection. She hung grimly on and hoped for the best, and all was, in fact, well.

All the beginners were told, in no uncertain terms, that when the trek was over, the interests of the pony came first and that, although stable girls were employed, the riders would have to help with the chores as part of their own training.

'I know that this is your holiday,' said the instructor, 'but we hope that you are all going to take up riding as a serious interest. If you do, you will probably have to look after a pony, which is not like a car, you know; you can't just get out and bang the door. You must look after your animal before you bother about yourself.' The instructor was an educated but no-nonsense type of woman. It interested Barbara that, as with hostelling, riding seemed to attract some people who regarded their own particular hobby as the be-all and end-all of existence. She began to wonder whether any of her clues would lead to a luxury holiday, sun-bathing on a beach miles away from energetic enthusiasts. Probably not – she was beginning to know her great-uncle by now. However, just as she had really enjoyed complying with the rules and the spirit of hostelling, so, rather to her own surprise, she found that she actually liked this imposed discipline. She was, therefore, a little surprised when one of the other girls did complain about it.

'It is all very well saying "I know that this is your holiday",' she exploded, 'but I don't want to work hard on my holiday; I work hard all the rest of the time.'

Barbara had some sympathy with that; after all, she was not on holiday exactly.

'May I talk to you about that in my office?' the instructor replied.

Barbara never discovered what was said in the office but she noticed that not only did the girl concerned never complain again but that she really began to enjoy the whole thing.

Each day their experience of riding and their understanding of their ponies – they always had the same one – increased, and by the Thursday they were actually trotting across the countryside, beautiful rolling hills and valleys, in which not a single pit-head or factory was to be seen. So much for her previous 'knowledge' of South Wales.

By now, it was very exhilarating and Barbara had seldom felt so happy.

Luckily, one of the others on the course, a girl called Brenda – why are so many more girls than men interested in riding? – was staying at the same guest-house, and they became friends fairly quickly.

'What first put you up to this lark?' Brenda asked one evening over dinner.

By then, Barbara felt that she knew Brenda well enough to tell her the whole extraordinary story; but, because she hated to sound superior, she pretended that the legacy was five – not fifty – thousand pounds.

'Lucky you,' said Brenda. 'Nobody is going to pay me five thousand quid for being here.'

'Perhaps nobody is going to pay it to me either,' Barbara commented, smiling. 'If one of these clues expects me to become a steeple-jack, or is there such a thing as a steeple-jill?, I am packing in. I would have to, I really can't stand much in the way of heights.'

'There is that,' Brenda agreed.

'But I'm lucky anyhow,' added Barbara happily. 'If it hadn't been for Uncle Tom's peculiar will. I would never had ridden a pony or even gone hostelling, I expect, and I'm jolly glad I have.'

'Guess why I'm here,' Brenda asked.

'Sorry. I should have asked.'

Barbara was very reluctant to risk sounding inquisitive.

'Well,' said Brenda, 'mine is not such a strange story as yours. It's just that I have bust up with my boy friend. I had been living with him for over six months and I've gone right off men for now.'

So that was another experience that Barbara had never had – and was never likely to. To her surprise, she felt a pang of envy, even though the affair had, it seemed, come to an abrupt end. She wondered why it had but did not like to ask.

'I'm sorry,' she said, not entirely truthfully.

It did not occur to Barbara that people tended to confide in her because they knew intuitively that she would not ask awkward questions that would make them regret having told her. It was also pretty clear that she could be trusted with confidences.

'You needn't really be sorry,' Brenda grinned cheerfully. 'It's happened before and I expect it will happen again. This trekking holiday – if it is a holiday – is certainly taking my mind off it.'

'In Victorian days,' asked Barbara, 'didn't men rush off to Africa and shoot things to forget about a girl?'

'So they say,' Brenda agreed, 'or they went on a Grand Tour of Europe. They must all have been bloody rich. But the books never say what happened to the girls who wanted to forget about a man, do they? They would not have been allowed to go abroad in those days all by their little selves, that's for sure.'

'No,' said Barbara, 'but I think that some of my clues will take me to Europe all by myself.'

'Good for you,' said Brenda, 'and all expenses paid.'

Rather to Barbara's surprise, Brenda then suggested that they went to the pub together, apparently it was a habit of hers, whereas to Barbara it was something rare and unusual. So, to her, a glass of cider in *The Lion* was quite an adventure in itself. Like so many near-teetotallers, she had no idea that cider is often stronger than beer and fortunately she did not choose vintage cider, which she might well have done.

Barbara was, in an odd sort of way that she could not begin to define, slightly shocked that Brenda drank beer. Barbara was still learning and was beginning to realize more and more fully just how little she had known about modern life before all this – she supposed that Brenda would have called it 'this lark' – had begun. It was certainly a lovely little country pub with most of the customers speaking Welsh.

The following afternoon, after Barbara and Brenda had finished their ride and seen to their ponies, they happened to see the next, much more senior, ride come back. It was led by a man and a girl looking radiantly happy. As the girl dismounted, she was greeted in a cross sort of way, by a young man leaning on a stick, who had apparently been waiting for her. The incident did not particularly register with Barbara, but that evening, at dinner, Brenda said,

'Poor girl. I bet she's lost him.'

Barbara looked completely blank.

'Lost whom?'

'The boy friend – the man with the stick we saw waiting for her this afternoon. He won't be pleased; those two looked so happy.'

The explanation, out of context, was a little cryptic but Barbara, by thinking very fast, understood it. She was still learning and reacting much more quickly to what people said.

The next day was tougher than before but there were only two days to go. They actually cantered in some quite wild country and it was really exhilarating. Just before the end of the ride, Barbara's pony stumbled and threw her. She had the curious sensation of flying very, very slowly through the air, not, curiously enough, frightening or unpleasant. Then, for the first time in her life, she saw stars – a whole constellation of them rather like, she thought in a dreamy kind of way, the stars on the United States flag. After that she fainted. She was dimly aware of being moved and of travelling somewhere in a very smooth-running vehicle, but she did not really come to her senses until she was safely tucked up in bed in a little cottage hospital.

'You are with us, are you?' said a smiling nurse. 'How do you feel?'

'I don't know yet,' Barbara replied in a small voice; and

then, after a pause, 'I fell off, didn't I?'

'You must have come quite a cropper – but nothing much seems to have been damaged – some bruises though and a bad sprain or two.'

'How long must I be here?'

'Probably only one night; we shall have to see what the doctor says.'

Barbara had a surprisingly good night, but suddenly awoke with a splitting headache.

Quite a young doctor came to examine her.

'You'll live,' he assured her cheerfully. 'You will probably feel a bit dizzy but you can get up soon. Take things easily for a couple of days. No more riding this week, of course.'

'But tomorrow is the last day of the trek,' said Barbara. 'I must ride if I possibly can.'

The doctor's eyes expressed his admiration, a delightful and unique experience for Barbara.

'Sorry, young lady,' he said, 'but I absolutely forbid it; doctor's orders.'

'Oh. All right then.'

The discipline that she had learnt on the riding course immediately stopped her from attempting to argue. You had to do what you were told. But she was disappointed, and she was pleased to find that it was a real disappointment, not just that she had failed to fulfil a clue. Once she had accepted the situation, she thoroughly enjoyed the rest of the day. It was a comfortable bed and she dozed off again.

She was allowed to go in the afternoon and was driven back to her guest-house. In the evening, she felt well enough to hobble out with Brenda to *The Lion*.

'Tough luck,' said Brenda 'I am sorry. Will you have to do another week to do what it said in that funny will?'

'I expect so,' Barbara replied, 'but I have so enjoyed it that I shan't mind.'

'It's not put you off then?'

'No,' said Barbara simply, and she was both pleased and surprised to realize that that was true.

'I missed you today,' said Brenda.

It was ages and ages since anybody had missed Barbara.

6

Barbara and Brenda travelled back to London, by rail, together. They duly exchanged addresses and made the usual insincere promises to keep in touch. It was very pleasant for Barbara to feel that she had made a new, even if temporary, friend so quickly. In the old days, she had never been able to do this. Two people doing something new together can easily become friends.

'I'm not a good letter writer,' Brenda admitted. 'If I don't reply if you write to me, it will be either because I am just plain lazy or because there is an instant new man – not that it seems likely at the moment; no time for letter writing then.'

Barbara could not attempt to match that excuse and simply smiled in acknowledgement.

The following day, she went, once again, to see James Garton, but not so cheerfully as on the previous occasion. She did not like failing at anything. Perhaps that was why she had so seldom tried.

'I don't think that this will count,' she informed James ruefully.

'Oh. Why not?'

'I didn't complete the course. I fell off.'

'Oh; I'm sorry. I did notice, of course, that you were limping when you came in but I thought it would be tactless to mention it. Are you all right otherwise by now?'

'Quite all right, thank you. I was only shaken and had a few bruises and sprains. I suppose I was lucky not to break anything.'

James was very surprised by the transformation in Barbara after so short a time. The serious, slightly severe 'Miss Lindley' whom he had first seen had not struck him as the sort of young woman who, a few weeks later, would make light of a bad fall.

His client had obviously guessed right; there was much more to Barbara than had appeared at first sight. How easy it is to misjudge people.

'I'm glad at least that it was no worse,' James said, 'and don't worry about the condition in the will. What you have done does count. The testator, I mean your great-uncle, did not specify any particular length of time for your riding; one day's trekking in Wales would in fact have satisfied the clue.'

'I would never have guessed that.'

'Of course you would not. It takes a lawyer's twisted mind to think like that.'

To avoid the slight embarrassment of being asked for them, Barbara handed over various papers in support of her account of the trekking and of the stay in hospital.

'I don't think that you need have any fears about solving future clues,' said James. 'The last one was, in my opinion, the most difficult of all to unravel. I was quite worried about it for you. I was told it was Welsh; but I borrowed a Welsh dictionary and I couldn't find it.'

'It may not have been there,' said Barbara, a little smugly, 'it's a modern word, I'm told. Mind you, I can't begin to imagine how Uncle Tom came across it.'

She then admitted to James that there had been a considerable element of luck in solving 'Merlota'.

'I suspect that it was not just luck,' James commented. 'There is such a thing as persistence. Congratulations.'

The next clue read:

'Spend a fortnight in Belgium and visit a town there which has given its name as a sort of title to several other towns, some of them in Great Britain.'

This turned out to be an easy one to solve. Barbara's experience with crossword-puzzles helped. She guessed that places that had a 'sort of title' would be double-barrelled names. She quickly dismissed 'Wells' but it led her to 'Spa', although it was news to her that the original town of that name was in Belgium.

As was, by now, her usual custom, Barbara spent a total of several hours in the library reading up the next 'subject' – Belgium in general and Spa in particular. She began to wonder if the library staff were at all inquisitive about what she was doing. Probably not; she was in London, after all.

Barbara had no particular fear of flying; but decided that she would prefer to go by rail and sea, via Ostend. As she wanted the early boat, she had to be on the train which left Victoria at eight in the morning for Folkestone. She was most intrigued that, near the end of the journey, the train reached a sort of terminus in the middle of nowhere and then reversed. She asked about that – she was finding it much easier now to speak to complete strangers – and was told that the drop down into Folkestone was so steep that the train had to execute a manoeuvre 'rather like a sailing boat tacking'. Or, as Barbara thought to herself, like some of the zig-zag paths on mountains.

There was something very romantic about a ship going to sea, particularly when flying the Blue Peter, the flag meaning 'I am ready to sail'. Trains have tracks and cars have roads, but ships are free. It seemed very definite when the engines slowly started and, first, a yard and then quite a distance separated the ship from the quay. It was a Belgian boat, so, in a way, Barbara was abroad already. As the sea was unusually smooth, Barbara risked having a full meal on board and enjoyed it very much. She had been quite childishly excited about going abroad alone for the first time and had not felt like eating any breakfast. Now it seemed very strange to see the coast sliding slowly past as she had lunch. She could still see the majestic rise of Dover Castle and was glad that it was a completely new route for her. It was fascinating that the first time any announcement was made, it was said in Flemish. There was a lot of shipping in the Channel and the North Sea so that Barbara was never bored.

As they approached Belgium, she was amazed by the extreme flatness of the low-lying Belgian coast. There was something rather attractively sinister about it – a sensation that she had felt once before on seeing the Thames on a grey day at Erith. Barbara thought, at first, that she had wrongly guessed where Ostend was because the ship sailed past the entrance to the harbour. However, she then gradually slowed to a stop and went carefully astern – or 'backwards' as Barbara thought of it, into the port, where she was dwarfed by menacing looking cranes. All the passengers then had to walk across a maze of railway lines to the customs sheds, which were so conspicuously decorated with flowers that it was a bit like being in a botanical museum. Her luggage was not examined in detail and she emerged into the station concourse. There she was surrounded by a large number of people, all completely indifferent to her and speaking in foreign languages. Noticing the Flemish spelling 'Oostende Kaai' for Ostend Quay she knew that she really was abroad, 'all by her little self' as Brenda had said, for the first time in her life. It was a strange sensation. With Brenda it would have been fun; alone it was a little frightening. Barbara had no difficulty in finding the train which would take her as far as Pepinster, where she would have to change. No wonder the French and others talk about 'mounting' a train; the platforms were not very high.

The first part of the journey was, as foreshadowed by her first sight of the coast, very flat indeed and very foreign looking. The tiny smallholdings, which seemed to be ubiquitous, gave a chess-board effect all through Flanders until nearly reaching Brussels. Barbara was intrigued by the curious name Erbs-Kwerbs as they passed rapidly through a little station. She was very puzzled that the train reached Bruxelles (Midi) before it reached Bruxelles (Nord); fortunately, it was not one of her clues to explain that. After the change into a slower train, the scenery for the remainder of the journey became more and more attractive and the last few miles were a delight. The train kept more or less parallel for miles – or did she mean kilometres? – with a rushing stream as it dashed its way through thick woodlands.

At Spa, Barbara got out a little map that she had been able to get in London and found her way on foot to the hotel. She found it difficult to deal with some taxi drivers in English and was not prepared to try the experiment in a foreign language. She reached a very attractive little inn after a few minutes walking.

One of the guide books that she had consulted had strongly recommended booking a room with a bath. That she had done, but she was surprised to find that she did not have, as she had expected, a private bathroom. The bath was in the bedroom and separated from the bed by a curtain only. However, that was good enough.

Barbara had arrived in very good time for the evening

dinner and, as it was a very pleasant warm evening, she went for a stroll in the little park, which had the odd name of 'Parc des Sept Heures'. She never did discover the reason for the title. It was a most attractive little park with delightful flowerbeds and bright green lawns. She returned, almost reluctantly, to the hotel and after a pleasant dinner, she went early to bed.

In her bedroom, all by herself, she felt for the first time, very lonely. Hostelling and riding had both taken her among people. This third clue had taken her, so far, alone and unprotected into a foreign land, where everything seemed strange. However, she soon fell asleep after the excitement of so much travel and so many new experiences all in one day.

She awoke feeling very nicely rested and keen to explore the little town. She was very glad that her great-uncle had directed her steps to a part of Belgium which was French-speaking. Ostend, with its Flemish, had inhibited her. Here she was able to practise her French; after all, she did have an A level in French and, for that matter, in German, and was pleased to discover that the Belgians spoke much more slowly than many French people, especially Parisians. She explored the town and when she felt that she could find her way around that, she went for an excellent little walk in the Ardennes countryside. It was mainly an enormous forest which, years later, she was to find that she much preferred to the better known Black Forest in Germany because here in Spa there was such an attractive mixture of conifers and deciduous trees. She was very pleased to find that Spa did not seem to be the sort of place to attract great crowds of foreign tourists. Indeed, after three days, she began to feel a little homesick, not having heard a single English voice. That was very surprising, because it was only a little out-of-season. Perhaps English tourists are very conservative and are reluctant to try little-known places. The feeling of being cut off from her own kind grew to such an extent that Barbara began to calculate the percentage of her time in Belgium that she had already passed – over twenty per cent done, less than eighty per cent to go! In hostels and in the riding school, she had never felt such an odd need. Here, she found it comforting.

On the evening of her fourth day in Spa, she noticed at

dinner a new arrival, at a table for one. It was a man just a little older than she. When he had finished his meal, he came over to Barbara's table and in an obviously English voice, said,

'Excuse me. You're English, aren't you?'

So much for Barbara's French accent.

'Yes.'

'So am I. May I join you for coffee, please?'

'If you wish.'

Barbara's manner, although not exactly frosty, was scarcely encouraging. She was simply shy and had no experience in dealing with sudden invitations. He looked nice enough, tall and fair-haired with grey eyes; but even if he had been very unattractive, Barbara had been taken by surprise and would have found it difficult to refuse.

'I am only here for two days,' he said. Perhaps he wanted to reassure Barbara that forty-eight hours would be the limit of his perhaps unwanted company. It reminded Barbara of Lynne, except that that had been the other way round; she had wanted to limit the length of Barbara's company!

'I am Peter, by the way – Peter Johns.'

'I am Barbara Lindley.'

'What a lovely name.'

'I like it too,' Barbara admitted, 'but I can't exactly take credit for it.'

'Are you on holiday?'

'Yes,' said Barbara. 'Are you?'

'Yes and no,' Peter replied enigmatically. 'I had some business to do in Brussels and it was all finished three days ahead of schedule. A friend of mine is always telling me how much he likes Spa, so I thought it might be worth a visit. Do you agree?'

'It certainly is a lovely little town,' Barbara replied. 'I keep meaning to make a day trip to Brussels or Bruges or Ghent; but I like Spa so much that I haven't left it yet.'

She could hardly say that she was very lonely at this stage in the conversation, which was a bit stilted. Barbara had had very little experience of talking to strange men and, more surprisingly, Peter was himself not exactly in his element in talking to strange girls. Indeed, he was pleasantly surprised at himself for starting this. We may or may not really be living in a permissive and 'hail fellow, well met' age, but there are still a

57

lot of gentle, courteous people around. In any case, Barbara would have been put off by a thick-skinned flatterer and would have seen him no more. With Peter, on the other hand, she soon felt at ease and not 'on duty', as it were, to prevent things getting out of hand.

'Have you seen the park yet?' Barbara asked.

'No, I have only just arrived, by taxi, from the station.'

'If you like,' said Barbara, 'I'll show it to you.'

'Thank you. I would enjoy that.'

It was surprising how much jollier the park looked now that she was showing it to a friend – well, a companion at least. She had known it only four days but already it had become 'her' park.

It was a lovely evening and as they passed a crazy-golf course Peter said,

'May I treat you to a round of that?'

'I don't know how to play.'

Barbara had always felt a little envious of people who had been able to pretend that they could do things which they had never tried and who, it seems, often got away with it. She could never do that.

'There is nothing to it,' Peter replied. 'That's why it's called "Crazy Golf".'

'OK then,' said Barbara.

Peter went to the little hut and emerged carrying two putters, two golf balls and two score-cards. For the next half hour, they directed the little balls, with varying degrees of success, over toy bridges and through miniature tunnels, across a little brook and past various gaily painted obstacles. At the eighteenth hole, the balls disappeared from sight, as if by magic, and Peter returned the putters. He had won by two strokes. Barbara was pleased; if Peter had contrived to lose, she would have noticed it at once and her simple happiness would have been spoiled. The lady who attended the kiosk which served the crazy-golf course said,

'Have you seen my dog?' She pointed to a large and friendly Bedlington. 'Is English dog.'

Barbara and Peter duly, and genuinely, admired him, said 'Good Night' and sauntered back to the hotel as the evening light was beginning to fail. Barbara had never sauntered alone.

When Barbara had reached her room, she sat on the side of the bed for a few minutes, just feeling happy. It was not, as she admitted to herself, an event of world-shaking importance, but she had really enjoyed that unexpected evening. She smiled a little ruefully to herself as she thought of the 'old' Barbara, the Barbara who had lived in the distant past that had come to an end three whole months ago. She could not have had that evening. She found herself wondering why, although really she knew the answer. First, of course, she would not have been in Spa; but, even if she had been for some odd reason, she felt sure that Peter would not have sprung his surprise invitation on her. She realized quite suddenly and clearly that, not only had she begun to live, but that the result of her doing so was to make her attractive to other people. It had not needed a man to show her that; actually Brenda had. But now, Peter too. She smiled happily to herself and started her bath.

Slightly to Barbara's surprise, she discovered the next morning that a table for two had been laid for her and Peter. She never did ask Peter whether he had arranged it or whether the hotel staff had decided, of their own initiative, to help things along. Although almost completely without experience of matters of this kind, Barbara was instinctively wise enough not to ask the wrong question.

'I would very much enjoy it,' said Peter, 'if you would show me round the town today.'

'All right,' said Barbara, and the slightly ungracious sound of the words was softened by her smile.

They wandered happily around the small town and then went for a little walk in the woods. There, they found a delightful open-air café-restaurant for a light lunch. They then resumed their walk and were startled to hear in a remote glade of the forest, a tinny voice, apparently coming from nowhere. It was rather like the sound of a distant gala or summer fête, which usually have an MC complete with megaphone. That impression was not far off the mark. Two minutes later, there came into view a curious little mini-bus with open sides and tiny wheels – rather like a mobile toast-rack writ large. It was pulling a trailer and the guide was giving a commentary.

They walked back to the town and decided to be lazy themselves in the late afternoon. They soon discovered where the little buses started from and travelled, at little more than walking pace, through the forest. It was a delightful and unusual ride.

Over dinner that evening, Barbara felt that, by now, she knew Peter well enough to tell him her curious story – but again substituting five for fifty thousand pounds.

'What a fascinating story,' said Peter 'I hope you win, if that is the right word.'

'So do I,' Barbara replied, 'but even if I don't, I'm very grateful to Uncle Tom. I have had more real fun in the last few weeks than in all the rest of my life put together.'

'I am very glad for you,' said Peter. 'It's so delightfully obvious that you are enjoying it so much. It makes me happy too.'

'Yes. I am enjoying it very, very much,' said Barbara. 'It's just that I now so wish that I had known Uncle Tom better when he was alive.'

'Didn't he come to visit you then?'

'Not very often, and when he did, I always got the impression that he did not approve of me very much.'

It did not occur to Barbara until very much later that her great-uncle and she were very much alike. If Uncle Tom had not suddenly and unexpectedly released her, she too would have become more and more reserved and acquired the feminine counterpart of her uncle's gruff manner.

'Your uncle has given you your freedom, hasn't he?' said Peter, and added, 'I wish I were a bit freer myself.'

'Oh?'

'I'm a bit tied up actually,' Peter explained. 'My mother, who is a widow, is partially disabled. She is very, very considerate and keeps saying that I must not feel bound, but I don't like to leave her alone any more than I must.'

'That is very good of you.'

'Oh, I don't know,' Peter admitted, 'I sometimes think, when I try to be honest with myself, that I may sometimes hide behind the situation. Perhaps it is an excuse for not branching out on my own.'

Barbara did not know Peter well enough, or his mother at all, to think of a suitable reply to that self-deprecating remark. And if Barbara could not think of the right reply to make, she very wisely kept quiet.

After dinner, they went once again to the crazy-golf in the park. This time, it was Barbara's turn to win. Fortunately, it did not need any great skill, and in any case, it did not matter at all who won. It was that kind of game.

They wandered back slowly to the hotel and had a final coffee together.

'There are several things that I would like to say,' Peter began, 'but I don't quite know how to say them. It boils down to saying that I have really very much enjoyed yesterday evening and today and I would very much like to meet you again in England.'

'Me too,' said Barbara.

Peter smiled happily but remained silent for a few seconds. Then he said,

'I shall miss you. Please write. I expect that you will have much more to tell me than I shall have to tell you. I really do want to know how you get on with this treasure hunt of yours – and everything.'

'I shall enjoy writing to you,' said Barbara. 'I agree that it will be easier for me, with so much to write about.'

'I am sure I am doing this very badly,' said Peter, 'but all I can do is to keep saying that I have enjoyed your company very much. You are a very nice person to be with and, whatever happens, I shall never forget you.'

It was not exactly a declaration of undying love, but Peter and Barbara were alike in this that they found any serious kind of 'romance' such a new and delightful experience that they did not altogether know how to deal with it, still less to talk about it. A more sophisticated kind of girl would have dismissed Peter out of hand and forgotten him the very next day. But Barbara was entirely satisfied. It was by far the nicest thing that had happened to her, ever.

The following morning, she got up fairly late. They had both agreed that they did not want a hurried farewell. It would have spoilt the leisurely leave-taking of the night before. So, when she came down to breakfast, Peter had gone.

Somehow, the idea of wandering around Spa or having local walks in the woods had lost its appeal; it would seem so empty without Peter. So Barbara decided to have excursions to Bruges and Ghent. She was enchanted by the Flemish architecture and by the quaint canals. Indeed, she had a boat trip on one of the canals. but she was surprised to find how flat it all seemed – not just actually flat but metaphorically flat as well, now that Peter was no longer there. She kept wanting to make comments to him about what she was seeing, but there was nobody there to hear them. Yesterday had been just perfect.

That evening she wrote a long letter to Peter including all the remarks she had wanted to make to him that day; a poor substitute but very much better than nothing. She also wrote to Edna. There would not have been much point in playing crazy-golf all by herself. She did mention Peter in her letter but, quite deliberately, played it down. As she re-read her letter, she wondered exactly why she had put it in so low a key. Partly, she did not want to show off by claiming to have acquired a boy friend, not that in modern parlance, he was exactly that – it was also partly that she did not wish to reinforce Edna's view that they were growing apart and, partly, as she admitted wryly to herself, that her old caution had not entirely disappeared. Peter had really enjoyed their time together, she was sure, but maybe he did not really want anything to develop and would quietly, but politely, drop her from his life. On the other hand, Barbara realized, a little to her own surprise – she was discovering many things about herself – that she did not want Peter to disappear from her life, especially not as suddenly as he had come into it.

The remainder of the fortnight, which included two day trips to Brussels, was very enjoyable in its way, but she continued to feel very lonely and isolated without Peter to share her interest. Still, she had been used to being alone for years, hadn't she? But she seemed, quite quickly, to have acquired a taste for company, clearly part of Uncle Tom's plan.

Like many women who had not been able to rely for years on a husband, Barbara was very competent with timetables and had armed herself, before leaving home, with Cook's Continental Timetable of Europe. So, instead of catching the big international express, she got up very early on the last day and travelled by an ordinary slow train to Ostend. Not only did this mean that she would be travelling with Belgians rather than with a lot of English tourists – and she was not very fond of tourists *en masse* – but she would arrive at the port ahead of the principal boat-train and could put her deck-chair where she wanted it before the driven hordes descended upon the ship.

As the train approached the coast, Barbara was interested to feel a slight sensation of excitement when she actually saw the sea. She must, she realized, have been somehow aware, without consciously noticing it, that the rails on which the train was travelling ran all the way from Vladivostok – or was there a change of gauge somewhere? – anyway, the continent was part of a huge land mass, quite unlike the British Isles. She realized for the first time that she was an islander. How odd!

The voyage back was quite rough and Barbara began to feel a little queasy. She had never been to a bar alone before but she knew that a small brandy – she always kept some at home for medical purposes – would put things right. So she did go down to the bar but was back on deck again, for fresh air, very quickly. The small drink – fortunately she disliked brandy, so it was unlikely to become a habit – had done what was expected of it and she thoroughly enjoyed sitting in her deck-chair and watching the white cliffs of Dover come gradually into view.

She had nothing to declare at the Customs and so went through the Green Channel. It was a strange sensation, because she found it difficult to decide whether to look straight ahead, which might look a bit as though she had something to hide, or to glance at the various Customs Officers, which might be construed as bluff. She did catch the eye of one of the Officers; but he just waved her on. Perhaps she looked as honest as she was?

The boat-train at Dover (Marine) Station looked surprisingly small compared with the Belgian trains. How odd after an absence of only a fortnight. She felt really at home at Victoria and even more so in her cosy little flat – particularly as there was, sitting on the mat, a welcome home letter from Peter.

7

Barbara was interested and surprised to find that, after all her strange wanderings, she was really looking forward to her fortnight's holiday with Edna. Her anticipated pleasure in it was reinforced by an odd conversation that she overheard in a bus.

'Where are you having your holiday this year, Jane?'
'Bournemouth.'
'When?'
'In ten days time, I hope, but I have got to go to Montreal and back first.'

The explanation of this curious exchange was, as Barbara discovered from their further conversation – you could hardly call it eavesdropping; they had such clear voices – that the girl looking forward to her stay in Bournemouth was an airline cargo pilot. Well, Barbara had not aspired to quite such heights, actually or otherwise, but her three clues so far had led her into such unknown fields, for her, that Eastbourne would be quite a change. Indeed, it would be something different in more ways than one; Edna, spurred on by Barbara's gallivants to unusual places, had decided to try somewhere different from Frinton this year.

They met at Victoria Station.

'You will have to give your boat-train a miss, this time,' said Edna.

'It's not exactly my boat-train,' Barbara smiled, 'and in any case I shall be glad to. Boat-trains are great fun, of course, but I am looking forward to our holiday in quite a different way.'

'I am looking forward to it too,' Edna agreed, 'but I hope it won't seem very dull to you.'

And then, she added, a little sadly, 'We have always enjoyed our holidays so much before.'

'Will you get it into your thick head,' said Barbara, smiling, 'that we shall this year. I have not become a different person, you know.'

'No,' Edna agreed, 'but all your jaunts recently have been so new and exciting, haven't they?'

'Well, yes: but, for heaven's sake, I don't want to live in a state of perpetual excitement. And, in any case, my journeys haven't been as weird as all that. Just something new and interesting.'

'Well, this is new at any rate,' Edna replied. 'You haven't been to farthest Eastbourne yet.'

It was on the tip of Barbara's tongue to say that in the Lakes, she had been to Far Easedale but she realized in time that that was a far more romantic name and indeed a far more romantic place. They enjoyed the train journey as they dashed along in Surrey and Sussex once London had been left behind.

They were both delighted by Eastbourne, although Edna, loyal to the last, maintained that Frinton was every bit as good, Eastbourne was an attractive town with the lovely front stretching all the way to the foot of Beachy Head. The air was most invigorating after London and the public gardens were bright with flowers of all kinds. They were intrigued to find that an old paddle-steamer was making some trips from the pier, and the excursion that they made on it was fascinating. They went down to a lower deck to watch the great pistons moving slowly and purposefully and gleaming with well-oiled brass, which gave a feeling of controlled power that no electric or internal-combustion engine could ever produce. They were so attracted by that that they went back to the top deck almost with reluctance.

During their stroll along the front that evening, Edna reverted to her apologetic mood.

'You are sure that you are enjoying yourself?' she asked.

'Look, Edna,' Barbara replied almost crossly, 'let's get this straight. I am enjoying this holiday very much.'

'You're not saying that just to please me?'

'No.'

'But you would have said that even if you hadn't meant it, wouldn't you?'

'I hope I would have tried,' Barbara admitted, 'but you should know me well enough by now to know when I really mean something.'

'Well, perhaps,' said Edna, not sounding very convinced.

Barbara did not press the matter. She could easily understand what it was all about. First of all, there was the fact that Edna had been doing a not very interesting job for months without a real break and then there was the fact of Barbara's own lucky escape from all that. Edna did not have to be a particularly envious kind of person to resent that just a little, even if only subconsciously. Barbara told her friend about the conversation in the bus between the girl pilot and her friend, and added,

'It's partly contrast and it's partly peace.'

'Peace?'

'Well yes, I am enjoying following out these peculiar clues of Uncle Tom's – and I expect the pilot enjoys her adventurous job – but it can be lonely at times. Also it is a bit exhausting really. I do value our friendship, you know.'

'So do I,' Edna agreed and then added rather wistfully, 'that's why I keep thinking that you will grow away from me.'

'Never,' said Barbara.

And she never did.

Barbara had not been lying, not even telling white lies. It was lovely just wandering about with Edna and sometimes having some pretty energetic walks on the Downs. They would never forget the view they had one afternoon from the top of Beachy Head when a very strong wind was blowing and the waves, crested with white foam, were dashing themselves against the lighthouse, striped in white and red, which looked for all the world like a toy perched on the rocks below.

On one of their rambles, they came across a riding school which advertised 'One day treks'.

'You would like to go on two of those, wouldn't you?' said Edna.

Taken by surprise, Barbara said,

'How do you know I would?'

Edna smiled.

'You told me the other day that I ought to know you by now,' Edna replied, 'and you are quite right, I do know you.

You missed two days after your fall, didn't you? You still think that you failed the riding clue.'

'Mr Garton seemed satisfied though.'

'You don't care two hoots what Mr Garton says, do you Barbie?'

Edna had become so enthusiastic that she had lapsed into the endearing form of Barbara's name that she had not used for ages. 'You think you failed; and you won't have if you go on two of those.'

'But you don't want to be left to your own devices for hours while I career about on a pony.'

'I shall not mind in the least,' Edna assured her friend. 'I like sitting on the beach and just watching the sea, and I know that you soon get fed up with that. So you see, it would suit us both.'

'OK. Thanks.'

Barbara was not entirely convinced by Edna's argument, and it also occurred to her that there would be nothing to prevent her from coming back to this or some other riding school, after the holiday. On the other hand, it would be nice to have it behind her. In any case, Edna would enjoy pleasing her – and she would be pleasing her; and all would be well again. And so, Barbara went on two of the treks on the Downs, one on each of their two weeks at Eastbourne.

Even on the first of those treks, Barbara was surprised to find that she felt quite at home in the saddle. It was quite a boost for her. Many of the people who went on the treks were real novices, just as Barbara had been so recently, but she found herself treated as though she were an old hand, a completely new and pleasing experience for her. She had never before been pointed out as an example of how to do a purely physical thing. She found it much more delightful to receive a compliment on a strange achievement than on something which was her own real speciality. Barbara had never really thought of herself as 'a rider'.

There was another aspect of the Sussex trekking that intrigued her. She had not set out for Eastbourne with any intention of going riding so she did not have her proper hat with her – her 'crash helmet' as she thought of it. Walking shoes and jeans were quite good enough for the trekking but she had no substitute for a hard hat. The riding school insisted on lending her one but Barbara could feel that it was too big and she knew very well that it would fall off her head if she fell and was really quite useless, if not positively dangerous. However, she was, by then, so keyed up and would have been very disappointed to have to cancel the ride that she said nothing about it. She would not voluntarily have ridden bareheaded, and what she was doing was, if anything, more dangerous, so she was being accidentally rather than deliberately foolhardy, and, to be honest with herself, she rather enjoyed it. She was pleased that she was, in a way, forced into taking a silly risk; quite exhilarating for someone who had been overcautious for far too long. She did not fall off and so all was well.

Both Barbara and Edna found the two evenings which followed the treks even more enjoyable than usual. Each had some news to tell to the other, but, as Edna remarked rather sadly,

'Once again, you have got more to tell me than I have to tell you.'

'As you keep harping on that subject,' Barbara replied pleasantly, 'why don't you join some sort of club or something?'

'I might.'

Barbara knew that she would have to be very careful. Edna was a little older than she and she had not had Barbara's stroke of good luck.

'Would I sound like a Dutch Aunt – if there is such a person,' she said, somewhat tentatively, 'if I talk some more about all this?'

'Go ahead,' said Edna. She was pleased really that Barbara was going to set the ball rolling.

'It is just that I have been very lucky,' Barbara began. 'I was very much of a stick-in-the-mud until Uncle Tom died and left his extraordinary will in my favour.'

'And you think that I am still a stick-in-the-mud?' Edna asked, but she smiled as she spoke. 'Well, you are quite right; I am.'

'That's half the battle,' said Barbara. 'Recognizing it, I mean. I had not realized that I was. It's difficult getting out of the rut, I know, but it is well worth it, and I am sure you can if you really want to.'

'Thanks for not just being polite, Barbara, and contradicting me. How am I supposed to get out of the rut then?'

'I don't know just what would suit you best, Edna, but since you ask me, think about it and do something about it. Do you know the old West Country adage; 'Do zummat. Do good if you can but do zummat'?'

'Actually, I think you are right,' Edna admitted. 'I'll spur myself on to do something positive as soon as this holiday is over. But no further arguments now, let's just enjoy it.'

And they did.

They were very lucky with the weather and they alternated lazy days – just town or beach strolling – with quite energetic days, walking on the South Downs. Whenever possible they had tea at Alfriston or in some other village and that refreshed them for the last three or four miles of their ramble. Their longest walk was to the Long Man of Wilmington, an enormous figure carved into the chalk hillside.

On the second Sunday, Edna said,

'I'm really grateful, Barbie, that you have set me such a good example and given me such good advice, but I don't see why it should all be one way round. Come to church with me this morning.'

'All right,' Barbara agreed, without much enthusiasm.

'It will be Eucharist.'

'What is that in English?'

'Sorry. Communion.'

'But am I allowed to go?'

'Certainly you are, but you can't actually take Communion.'

'Won't it look odd?'

'No, no, there are nearly always some people who don't.'

It was rather a high church service, but Barbara, to her surprise, actually enjoyed it. The lovely words of the Eucharist rolling down the aisle, the excellent singing and all the colours in the beautiful old church really delighted her.

'Thank you, Edna,' she said afterwards. 'I'll give church a second chance if that does not sound patronizing.'

'No, of course not. You may have been unlucky in the ones you tried before.'

'I certainly was.'

'The worst I ever came across,' said Edna 'reminded me of a story somebody told me about a little girl. She was usually very chirpy and she was taken by an aunt to a church that the girl had never been to before. On the way home, the small girl was unusually quiet.

' "Are you all right, dear?" the aunt asked. There followed a long pause until, at last, the girl said, "Does your Vicar say actual words?" "Of course, he does," the aunt replied. But the little girl said, "Ours doesn't. He says 'Wah, wah, wah, wah, wah' all the time." '

Barbara agreed that that criticism could not be levelled at the church service in Eastbourne.

'I would find Sundays very shapeless if I did not go to church.' Edna said. 'I really enjoy it.'

Barbara was very impressed. She had always thought that people went to church as a duty.

They were both genuinely sorry when the holiday came to an end.

'Thank you, Barbie,' Edna said at Victoria. 'I enjoyed that holiday more than ever before, and I had thought that I would like it less.'

'There is something to be said for not looking forward to anything too much,' Barbara said. 'You are a very nice person to be on holiday with. Bear that in mind in your cogitations about what you are going to do about things, won't you?'

Barbara let herself into her little flat, feeling very happy. Edna had very much enjoyed the Eastbourne holiday, and so, rather to her own surprise, had she. For her friend, the simple change of place and Barbara's companionship had been enough; for Barbara it had been lovely just to have a peaceful holiday for once. It had been so considerate of Edna to suggest the two days riding. Nobody else would have guessed that Barbara had still felt that she had not fulfilled the 'merlota' clue. She really detested any kind of cheating – even where, as here, it was a legitimate wangle. Anyway, she had actually enjoyed the trekking, she really had and it was true that, unlike Edna, she soon got tired of sitting on a beach.

In days gone by, when Barbara had returned from one of her holidays with Edna, she would have been going back the next day to the start of a long period of work in the office. Now it was quite different. What would the next clue be? She did so hope that it would not turn out to be quite impossible, but, even if it did, it would not matter all that much. She had gained a confidence now that would last her all her life. What she wondered, was this kind of confidence? She recalled that once, in a train that had stopped at a station mainly to pick up schoolchildren, she had noticed, when the train was just due to depart, that a girl was sauntering along the platform on the opposite side of the line. She crossed the footbridge, but without running. It was a small incident, but Barbara had thought, at the time, that the girl showed a confidence that all would be well. Now, perhaps, Barbara had acquired confidence too. Nobody was likely, ever again, to refer to her as a 'poor dear'. How long ago that seemed and wasn't it lucky that she had overheard that remark after and not before she had accepted Uncle Tom's challenge?

8

The next morning, she set out once again to get instructions from James Garton who by now and at her request had dropped the formal 'Miss Lindley'.

'Good morning, Barbara,' he said. 'Did you have a good holiday?'

'Yes. It was great, thank you.'

'And your friend?'

Barbara smiled.

'Oh, yes. She said that it was the best we had ever had. I would not have enjoyed it so much myself if she hadn't.'

'Good,' said James, with an enigmatic smile. 'That's another clue satisfied.'

'I have no idea what you mean.'

'Of course you haven't,' James agreed, 'but one of the conditions, not in fact disguised as a clue, was that you should give somebody else a treat.'

'But, but I haven't. I've just had a treat myself.'

'That is sometimes the best way to do it.'

'But what a funny clue – I mean condition,' Barbara said. 'I thought that they all had to do with being adventurous.'

'Well, this one did not,' James agreed, 'but I don't think that it was particularly odd. I quite got to like the old gentleman and I think that I even began to understand him at our second meeting. He had worked out a lot of adventurous things for you to do, and then he thought for a bit and came up with the idea of a treat for somebody else. He added, "I don't just want Barbara to be outgoing for her own sake; I want her to be a good person as well." That is why he thought of that one. I am glad that I did not have to put it up to you as a condition and ask for some evidence such as a signed statement from your friend saying "I hereby certify that I have enjoyed myself".'

'Well, well,' said Barbara. And she felt that she liked her great-uncle more than ever before. But to become 'a good person' was rather a tall order. Wouldn't it be nice if she succeeded at that!

'It seems such a small thing to have done,' Barbara added.

'It is surprising how such small things can matter,' James commented. 'I remember reading once about a foreign prime minister who had decided to appoint a particular man to high office. Before the appointment was published, the PM saw the man concerned sitting in a train next to an elderly woman who was standing. The man made no attempt to offer her a seat. The PM cancelled the appointment.'

After a short pause, because Barbara was obviously thinking, James handed her the next clue.

All it said was:

'Act now.'

'I think I can guess what this is supposed to mean,' Barbara said, 'but I am not quite sure.'

'Hm,' James said, 'I'm afraid that you will have to do what you think it means before I am allowed to tell you whether you are right or not. Silly isn't it? But if you are wrong, I can explain some more. But I expect you have guessed right.'

For some reason that James could not begin to guess, Barbara suddenly looked very solemn.

'Are you in a hurry to get rid of me this morning?' she asked.

'Not at all, I have no other appointment for twenty minutes.'

There was a short silence.

'My little sister,' Barbara began, and stopped.

'I'm sorry,' she resumed. 'She died when I was ten but I like to think about her sometimes. She was very fond of asking us to guess things, but if we guessed too quickly, and the answers were sometimes pretty obvious, she used to say, 'And now guess if you have guessed right.' It's a bit like that now, isn't it?'

'Yes,' said James, simply.

As Barbara went out into the morning sunshine, she thought: This is the first indoor adventure; I had expected that they would all test physical stamina or skill. Then, quite suddenly, she felt very sorry about her little sister of whom she had, by chance, been so suddenly reminded. Just mentioning her to James had brought it all back and Barbara felt rather ashamed that her first thought, on leaving the solicitors' office had been about her next clue. Claire, her sister, had been only eight when she died. It had been a terrible shock for Barbara because her parents had not had the forethought to warn her. They had known that it would happen before long but Barbara too had been a child at the time, so her parents had kept silent in the mistaken belief that they were protecting her. They had not told Claire herself either but, looking back, Barbara had the odd feeling that, somehow, without being told, Claire had known all the time. Quite suddenly, Barbara stopped feeling sad and started, in an odd sort of way that she could not begin to define, to feel actually happy about her as though she now knew, for the first time, that all was well with Claire.

Reverting to her own situation, Barbara was surprised to discover that she was very frightened about the next clue. So far, she had been asked to do things which, in a vague sort of way, she had envied other people for doing. But, acting – not only had she never wanted to act but she seriously doubted her ability to succeed. Even at school, she had consistently dodged having to appear on a stage. Why, she wondered, were different people alarmed by such different things? However, although by now thoroughly worried about it, she applied herself, in her usual methodical way, to working out how best she could at least attempt to fulfil this clue. She went home to read the advertisements in the local paper and then kept her eyes open for play bills by amateur local groups. She discovered that there would be three productions in the next fortnight.

One evening she went to the first of the three plays, but she was so daunted by the high standard of the acting that she went home thinking, 'I could never do that.' The second one that she tried was good but not so startlingly good as the first. There was a little footnote to the programme which read:

'We are always on the lookout for new members with or without previous experience. If you are interested, please ring John at 731 6825.'

The very next day, before she developed cold feet and gave up the whole idea as hopeless, Barbara plucked up courage to telephone the mysterious 'John'. It was going to be difficult enough to push herself forward in this unprecedented way without what was to her the additional hurdle of a telephone call to a man who had not revealed his surname. Suppose that she became tongue-tied on the telephone. She would hardly be welcome, after that, she thought, in a drama group. However, all went in accordance with plan and she was invited to present herself at a little hall on the following Thursday.

Following her usual practice of arriving much too early, Barbara was somewhat put out to find that the hall door was locked. After she had paced up and down for at least five minutes, a man arrived and unlocked the door.

'Good evening,' said Barbara. 'Are you – er John?'

'Yes. And you are?'

They had obviously not been waiting on tenterhooks for her important arrival!

'Barbara Lindley.'

'Oh yes. You rang me last week. Welcome to the group.'

Notwithstanding the words he used, he did not sound particularly pleased to see her. Was there something about her to make him decide that she would be no good at acting?

It was a very stuffy and somewhat dusty hall with the usual musty smell of poorly kept wooden buildings. Gradually, several more people arrived, mostly in pairs. Then John called them all together and, in a rather offhand way, introduced Barbara as a new member of the group.

'Right,' John barked, 'we'll start with our usual movement exercises.'

Barbara got the clear impression that John was a sergeant-major manqué. Did they not all start speaking by using the meaningless word 'Right'? Indeed, Barbara felt that John would much rather have said,

'Fall in. Wake up. You're all half asleep,' and that it was only the fact that this was a group of volunteers that modified his words and manner to some extent.

Barbara soon found that she had to do exercises of a kind that she had not done since leaving school and had no particular wish to do again. She did not quite see the point of it all and John did not see fit to enlighten her.

After about half an hour of PE – or so it seemed to Barbara – they broke off for coffee. Barbara still felt very awkward about all this – particularly as nobody else had, so far as she could see, answered the appeal for new members. Certainly, she was the only girl not wearing a leotard; the men were less uniformly dressed. It looked as though she would have to wear yet another type of kit for this new clue. She would have quite a wardrobe by the time it was all over.

Everybody seemed to know everybody else, except her. Nobody made any real attempt to make her feel welcome. On the other hand, nobody was positively discourteous to her, and one girl actually congratulated her on the way she had done the movement exercises, a rather grander name than PE. Apart from that, the others made the occasional meaningless polite remark to her, but showed no real interest in her arrival. Barbara got the clear signal that this was a tightly-knit group and that, subconsciously or otherwise, they resented new arrivals. Why then had they positively advertised for them? Soon after coffee, the explanation became clear. They had provisionally planned to produce a play called 'Zack' in two months time and one or two small parts had not yet been filled. Would Barbara like to play the maid in the next production? John attempted to make this sound like a grand and generous offer rather than a plea for help. With an odd mixture of relief that her part would presumably be a small one and slight resentment that she had been more or less thrust into this rôle, Barbara agreed without demur. Why not get it over with?

The group – it called itself 'The Milbourne Players' – met twice a week. Barbara had her lines to learn and she decided to learn them all before the next rehearsal. She found it very difficult at first and, typical Barbara, she made her way to the librry for a book about acting. The book recommended the use of tape-recorder. With the aid of that, she did find it much easier to practise her lines and to commit them to memory, like a gramophone record. At the end of four days, and, after all, she had nothing else specific to do, she was convinced that she knew all her lines. It was, therefore, very disappointing for her that, at the first rehearsal, she needed four prompts. It did not, in fact, matter because all the others were simply reading their parts. Indeed, John, with obvious reluctance, congratulated her on so nearly knowing her lines so soon.

'Nobody can learn lines perfectly at home,' he admitted. 'You have got to say them to the right person and get your clues from the right person too.'

It seemed so odd to Barbara to have so little to do; she could hardly recite her lines for sixteen hours a day. So she rang James to ask whether it would be permissible to start her next clue at the same time.

'Sorry, no,' James told her. 'I did suggest that myself to your late great-uncle but, for some reason, he was quite adamant on the point. There would have been no purpose in arguing. You will have to finish your present clue first.'

So, for the first time since she had left school – and then only in the holidays – Barbara found herself with too much time and too little to do in it. She read a lot and went for an occasional country walk alone, but she nevertheless began to feel a little bored. For the first time ever, she began to understand why some retired people become restless and inactive. Barbara felt a little ashamed of herself. She remembered reading an article in a magazine which proved conclusively that boredom was a vice which could be avoided. Perhaps Uncle Tom had that in mind and was forcing her into a position where she would have to do something about it, with no clear guide-lines.

Bearing that in mind, she decided to invite Edna to her flat one evening and used part of her unusual leisure in cooking a really good meal. She actually bought a rather elaborate cookery book – did Barbara ever start anything without the aid of a book? – and enjoyed selecting and preparing a splendid little dinner for her friend. Edna was very flatteringly surprised by the meal and, helped a little by two glasses of table-wine – like Barbara she was almost a teetotaller – she really opened up.

'Barbie,' she began 'may I really talk to you?'

Barbara realized at once that this was a serious beginning and resisted any temptation to make a jocular remark about the odd wording. That would have stopped everything dead in its tracks.

'Of course, Edna, as long as you like.'

'I don't suppose that I'll talk much sense,' Edna began, 'I'm really only thinking aloud. I'm thirty-one now and nothing much of interest has happened to me. Somehow, I didn't realize that until all this happened to you. I simply must make something happen, but I don't know where to start. I know that there are bureaux, if that is the right word, for friendship and marriage and things like that, but it would seem like putting myself up for auction somehow. What do you think?'

'I think you are probably wrong about the auction idea – if the bureau is a good and well-established one, but why not keep that scheme in the background to start with and have a go all by yourself first? But if you do, promise yourself that you'll try the "contact" idea if you don't get anywhere without it.'

'Why do you want me to promise it?'

'We are both very much alike really,' Barbara answered, 'and we both find it easier if there is an escape route somewhere – or do I mean if there is not an escape route somewhere?'

Barbara paused and smiled.

'I'm expressing myself very badly,' she resumed. 'I'll try again. What I am trying to say is that the contact bureaux would give you a second chance, but that if you promise in advance, then you won't be able to escape trying if necessary. And, if you don't want to be forced into that in the end, you will have more of an incentive to succeed all by yourself. I do hope that that is a bit clearer?'

'I see exactly what you mean. All right, I promise.'

'Good. Have you any bright ideas for a start?'

'Well, I did wonder about amateur acting.'

'Oh' said Barbara.

'You don't sound very enthusiastic.'

'Sorry,' Barbara said. 'It may be a very good idea. It is just that I wouldn't recommend my lot. They are not a very friendly group. What put you on to this?'

'Another girl in the office. She started last year with a drama class that puts on two plays a year.'

'A class might be very different,' Barbara conceded. 'You will all be in it from the start. I'm a sort of unwelcome latercomer. Your idea is well worth a try.'

'I thought so too, but I am a bit put off by your experience.'

'I'm sorry. But look, Edna, I have been simply pitchforked into play-acting as you very well know. In any case, a class with a proper tutor is a very different kettle of fish. But, even if acting is not in my line, it may very well be in yours.'

Edna suddenly smiled.

'I was good at it at school.'

'Well, there you are then. I was always frightened of the stage. I still am.'

'You've got more courage than I have,' said Edna.

'Try it and see.'

'I don't see how it can possibly be a bad idea,' Edna persisted, 'even if it is not actually a good one. Can I keep ringing you up and telling you how I'm getting on?'

'Of course you can, and I hope very much that the scheme works,' Edna suddenly looked much braver and more determined than Barbara had ever seen her look before.

'There will be troubles all right,' she said. 'It's just that I shall find it difficult to accept them and to - er - win through, I hope. Oh dear, doesn't that sound like something from an improving magazine?'

'And I don't want to sound like a governess,' Barbara responded, 'but would it help if you promised me to join the class?'

'You do know me, don't you Barbie? Very well then, I promise.'

During the following few weeks, Edna duly started her drama classes and Barbara persisted with the rehearsals. This remained the first of her clues that Barbara did not enjoy doing. She just did not fit in with these people. It struck her as very odd that this was so, because superficially, they were more like her than most of the people she had met at hostels and in the riding school, or so she had thought, but she was really not enjoying these rehearsals one bit and was still alarmed by the prospect of a public performance.

Barbara clearly began to realize that one of the things that was happening to her was that she was discovering more and more about herself; not by indulging in introspective thought - heaven forbid - but by really experiencing things at first hand. It certainly still mystified her that she was genuinely afraid of acting but had not been particularly worried that she might fall off a pony or that, having done so, that she might fall again. It seemed daft to her, but, try as she might, she could not visualize herself as a real actress on a real stage in front of real people.

Strangely enough, the exact opposite seemed to be happening to Edna. She met Barbara from time to time and was clearly enjoying her drama course. Barbara was really pleased that Edna seemed to be succeeding where she herself was – well, not exactly failing, she hoped, but certainly unhappy and nervous about the whole thing. It was not only that she was terrified of drying up on the stage or of making a fool of herself in some other way. It was more that she felt excluded from the so-called Group and was very hurt because the producer not only kept nagging her to play the part of the maid as something of a minx but had said, after three rehearsals,

'Oh well. I don't suppose you can do it any better. Forget it.'

And he never again pursued the point, giving her up as hopeless as an actress.

This was a very odd period in Barbara's life and it was a pity that she had so much time alone in which to brood. The producer's unkind remark kept going round and round in her head, and the more it did so the more she felt hurt by it. This was strange. She didn't want to be a minx, did she? Why on earth then did she so much resent the remark? The dress rehearsal was very flat indeed and Barbara went home feeling quite depressed. At least, she had staggered through her lines without any mistakes. And still she had not succeeded in working out why she was so troubled by the producer's comment.

On the day of the first performance, she felt very isolated in the dressing-room; several of the others had 'Good Luck' cards or sometimes, for superstitious reasons, what amounted to 'Bad Luck' cards on display. Also, Barbara was, to her extreme fury, beginning to tremble. Even worse, when, at long last, she was in the wings waiting for her cue to go on stage, she shook like an aspen leaf – at least, that was what it felt like – and her mouth started to go very dry. The time for her first appearance got nearer and nearer and finally arrived. With a courage far exceeding that which she had ever before had to deploy, she went on stage and said her first line. Then, immediately, everything seemed to change. The producer was now effectively gagged and was no longer able to make his sarcastic comments to her. There was only a friendly audience waiting to enjoy the play, hidden away in a dark pit at her feet. Almost a minor miracle occurred.

'I'll show him,' she suddenly thought, although in reality it was a feeling rather than anything which could properly be described as a thought.

What did he mean by saying, 'I don't suppose you can.' I jolly well will. And with that feeling, she turned, very temporarily, into a minx. The effect was quite galvanic. She felt quite different. She was, for a few minutes, a completely different character, and the audience loved it. When the performance was over, three of the cast, who had much larger parts, genuinely congratulated her. They were generous enough to realize that, like many others before them, they had underestimated Barbara. However, most of the others seemed rather annoyed. They had not expected her, Barbara of all people, to come up from behind and steal some of their thunder.

'I always said you could,' the producer declared, and it was a blatant lie.

There were three performances, and the world seemed to restart after it was all over.

Barbara had not experienced anything quite like that since doing A levels. Then, as now, the whole purpose of life seemed to have been fulfilled – the examination papers written, the play performed. She had not visualized any future afterwards so, when she awoke after the night of the last performance, she felt that a new lease of life had been unexpectedly granted to her. She felt delightfully free, as though she had nothing to do at all but wander about. She could even forget her lines. She was quite happy to forget most of the members of the group. She had made no friends there. Nevertheless, it would have been churlish to refuse the invitation to go to the little celebration party the following weekend. When Barbara had hesitated, one of the girls had said, 'But we always have a party after a play and everybody comes to it.'

So Barbara had rather reluctantly agreed. It was to be held in a flat of one of the more affluent members of the cast.

Even preparing for it presented a slight difficulty to Barbara. She was expected to bring a bottle of wine as her contribution. She quite forgot about that until she had actually set out for the party. All the general stores were shut and, strangely enough, she had never been inside an off-licence. She almost had to force herself to enter. Why she thought that something weird might happen to her there, Barbara could not herself have explained. Thinking about that, she recalled how, as a child, she had read something in a newspaper about attacks on people in Liverpool. She remembered that on one occasion she had travelled there alone and she had supposed that at least two men complete with knives would be stationed immediately opposite each carriage door. No such threats had in fact materialized. Neither, so many years later, did anything alarming happen in the off-licence.

As usual, she arrived early for the party but she had not realized that people going to London parties tend to arrive well after the advertised time. Indeed, when Barbara arrived, she found that she was expected to help get the sandwiches ready. She was surprised but glad to do so. When she or Edna visited one another, the guest certainly expected to find everything ready and waiting. However, these people were rather more Bohemian. After a while, the others gradually trickled in, without any apology for lateness and Barbara began to feel a bit happier with these, to her, strange people – well, with some of them anyway – than she had ever done before. The party became extremely jolly and noisy, but, with the aid of some wine, Barbara was able, to some extent, to enter into the atmosphere of fun and relaxation. Although it was by now nearly eleven o'clock, people were still arriving (for a party advertised as 'at about eight') and nobody seemed inclined to leave, which was awkward because Barbara had a horror of seeming discourteous. She was sitting quietly for a few minutes still wondering whether it would be rude to go at midnight, when she recalled a story about Charles Lamb in the days when he still worked in an office. He had been chidden for arriving late and had replied, 'But see how early I leave.' Barbara hoped that, contrariwise, she would not be expected to leave very late notwithstanding her early arrival. Armed by the pleasant recollection of the little story, Barbara smiled. A young man, Bob, another member of the cast, caught the smile and assumed that it was intended for him (some young men are very conceited) and it is women, thought Barbara, who are supposed to be vain. However, she could hardly say, 'But I was not smiling at you,' so they chatted quite happily about the play – the only topic that they had in common.

'Are you joining the group permanently, Barbara?'

'No,' said Barbara, so abruptly that she felt herself blushing by way of apology for her unaccustomed rudeness, accidental though it had been, and she tried to soften her remark by adding,

'I am going to be very busy with a lot of other things.'

'So you are leaving us?'

'Yes.'

'Just as I was getting to know you.'

'Er,' was all that Barbara was able to say.

'Well, at least let me say "Good-Bye".'

Barbara could not see any particular reason why he should not say 'Good-Bye' but it sounded as though he was asking permission. How odd!

She was not in the least prepared for what he said next.

'Would tomorrow evening suit you?'

'I'm sorry?' said Barbara, bewildered.

'Please let me take you out for a farewell dinner.'

'Oh,' said Barbara, not very enthusiastically but, influenced perhaps by the wine and the background noise she added, 'Er, thank you.'

To her annoyance she blushed again, but duly wrote down in her little diary where and when they were to meet. She then thanked her hostess and fled into the night.

Barbara was worried. She felt that she had been bounced into accepting the completely unexpected invitation. If that had happened two months earlier she would have been quite terrified of the unknown. She was still a little frightened of it. Quite apart from that, she felt that she was being disloyal to Peter. She realized that she was being over-scrupulous; after all, she was not engaged to him. Nevertheless, the feeling persisted, however illogical it might be. As she went over and over all this in her mind, she discovered an odd thing: it was less disturbing to have two things to worry about than one.

Whenever she felt herself obsessed by a feeling of disloyalty to Peter, she switched to thinking how difficult and possibly embarrassing the dinner date was going to be. At least it made a changed channel for her worries. It never once occurred to Barbara to cancel the meeting. She had agreed to it, hadn't she? Fortunately, she did not have many days in which to worry on either count.

So, two days later, she put on a very pretty flower-patterned dress and set off. Bob was waiting for her and greeted her effusively.

'Let's have a drink first,' he said.

Without waiting for a comment, he almost propelled Barbara into a very noisy pub. Guessing, correctly, that she would be offered wine at the dinner, she insisted on tomato juice as an apéritif. She also thought, again correctly, that this might give Bob a hint at an early stage that this was to be a one-off meeting. They did their best to discuss the play – a rather exhausting effort because of the background din.

Barbara was pleased to be in the open air again; not, however, for very long, because less than five minutes later, she found herself being led into a posh Italian restaurant.

Almost immediately, a waiter appeared and asked,

'Would you care for dinner?'

Bob just replied, 'Yes please,' but Barbara would have been tempted to say, 'No, I came in here for a pair of shoes.' She did not like nonsensical sycophancy. On the other hand, as she admitted wryly to herself, she would not have had the nerve actually to make her imagined reply.

Barbara could not complain, however, about the meal or the ambience; both were superb.

At the coffee stage Bob said,

'It's still quite early. Shall we go to my place?'

'No.'

Barbara's reply was almost an explosion. Her worst fears were being realized, but even at that time, she knew that her reply must have sounded so definite as to be positively rude. She started to blush and wished that the floor would disappear and she with it. After what seemed an age to her, she glanced at Bob to see how he was reacting. She could have refused without being so rude. To her relief and surprise, however, Bob was smiling in a most attractive way. Was that a softening-up process for a second attempt?

'I'm so sorry that I sounded so abrupt,' said Barbara, 'but really, no thank you.'

Bob continued to smile in an enigmatic way.

To break the silence, Barbara, still feeling very embarrassed, said,

'What is so funny?'

'Me, I think,' Bob replied.

'I thought perhaps it was me,' Barbara admitted.

'No, really not,' said Bob in a much more sincere voice than he had ever used before. 'Thank you for telling me so clearly that it is no go.'

As he seemed to have accepted defeat very graciously, Barbara felt that she could risk being more courteous.

'It probably is me who is so funny,' she confessed. 'You see, I'm really not used to this sort of thing and you took me completely by surprise.'

'That's quite OK,' said Bob, 'I rather like to know how the land lies.'

'But I am sorry if you are disappointed, really.'

'In a way. I am not,' said Bob. 'You can't win them all.'

'Well, anyway,' said Barbara, 'I feel a bit of a fraud. I should not have accepted your invitation.'

'Rubbish, Barbara. I am enjoying this evening, even though it is not a lead-up to a night.'

Barbara did not quite know what to say to that. It was not the sort of remark that she was used to.

'You are sure?' she asked after a pause.

'Quite sure, I've surprised myself a bit, but I am sure. So, as a cosy evening in my flat is ruled out, what about a walk in the park?'

Barbara looked a little uncertain and said only,

'Er . . . '

'Don't worry.' Bob smiled at her. 'I won't try anything on: I promise.'

'I should love a walk in the park.'

They wandered into Hyde Park and sat for a while watching the fountains play in the evening sun. Then they strolled on to Kensington Gardens and the Round Pond.

'Are you enjoying this?' Barbara asked, a little tentatively.

'If you are?'
'Yes.'
'Well, I am very much.'
'Thanks for the compliment.'
Then, after a pause, she added
'Well, it is nice, isn't it?'
'It is, and I am very glad that you believed what I said,' Bob commented.

'Well,' Barbara smiled, 'I usually know when somebody can be relied on, but I still feel that I may have misled you by coming at all.'

'Not in the least. And in any case, it makes a pleasant change. I am really enjoying just this evening.'

They strolled on in silence for a minute.

'What do you do for a living?' Bob asked.

'Nothing at the moment.'

'Oh, I am sorry.'

'Now I have misled you,' Barbara admitted. 'You need not be sorry at all; quite the reverse in fact. I'll tell you all about it.'

When Barbara had finished a brief account of what had happened so far and of what the future might be, Bob said,

'That is one of the most amazing stories I have ever heard. So that is why you joined our little group.'

'Yes.'

'You don't picture yourself as a future actress with your name in lights?'

'Not at all. No, sorry. But thank you for even thinking of it as a possibility.'

'But you did your part very well indeed.'

'Yes,' said Barbara, smiling. 'I did, didn't I? But I don't quite know why or how. I think somehow that I was fed up with the producer, and when he suddenly wasn't there – at least he was, but I couldn't see him – I suddenly felt – oh, I don't know – free I suppose.'

'Yes. I think that makes sense.'

Barbara was almost sorry when they emerged into Kensington High Street, or High Street, Ken, as Londoners usually call it, and she was quite happy to go into a pub, but she was still just a little cautious and had another tomato juice.

'If I were you,' said Bob, 'I would put in a little practice with booze.'

'Whatever do you mean?'

'Well,' said Bob, 'I expect you will meet some other scoundrels.'

'I shouldn't mind,' Barbara admitted, 'if they are all as kind as you have been this evening.'

'This is an evening for compliments,' said Bob. 'I must try this sort of thing again some time. It has felt kind of peaceful for a change.'

As they approached the underground station, Barbara said,

'Well. This is "Good-bye" isn't it?'

'I don't usually ask this,' said Bob, 'but is it in order to ask for a good-night kiss?'

Barbara just smiled and nodded.

What an interesting and unusual evening; and she had not been looking forward to it one bit.

9

When Barbara went once again – it was becoming quite a habit – to see James Garton, she was assured that her next clue would not involve anything particularly difficult, just a lot of travel, and further from home than usual.

The clue read:

'Where is the Cheese-cutter Bridge? Use a train over water to get there. Spend a fortnight in Scandinavia altogether.'

It was not particularly difficult to discover the whereabouts of a train-ferry, but it took a lot of research in libraries and in the offices of travel agents to find any information about the 'Cheese-cutter bridge'. Barbara was quite happy in libraries but she felt almost fraudulent when enquiring of travel agents whose services she might not use. Fortunately, this particular clue came up late in Spring and Barbara prepared for the holiday with considerable pleasure. She had enjoyed complying with the difficult clues even when, as had happened with the acting clue, the enjoyment had come only at the end. However, it was nice once again to look forward to a journey on which she could relax without wondering whether or not she would be able to do what was expected of her at the end of it.

Clearly part, but only a part, of Uncle Tom's plan was that she should travel widely. It was very considerate of the old gentleman to have arranged that when she went abroad she had nothing difficult to do. Going abroad or doing something difficult in Great Britain seemed to be the plan, but she was not expected to tackle both together. Barbara had a great deal of sympathy with RL Stevenson's view that it is better to travel hopefully than to arrive. She thoroughly enjoyed making all the preparations, including getting different kinds of foreign currency.

The day for departure came. She arrived very early at Liverpool Street Station and, once she had discovered the correct platform for the boat-train, she had a very leisurely cup of coffee. She always found it a pleasant contrast to have nothing to do after working hard, especially when, as here, there was no duty or temptation to look for something to do. She came to the conclusion that the station must have been designed originally when the architect was drunk, so oddly was it planned, if that was the right word for the maze of subways and bridges.

The ship was waiting at Parkstone Quay (Harwich) and Barbara went straight to her cabin. She was to share it with a completely unknown woman and, just as she had preferred to arrive at her first hostel ahead of everybody else, so, here too, she was glad that the cabin was empty when she reached it. She was intrigued to see how compact everything was. It was all very cosy, with not a cubic inch of space wasted. She began to wonder what her companion would be like, but she was not unduly worried because the voyage would be over in nineteen hours.

A few minutes later, a fair-haired, cheerful looking girl of about twenty-five sailed into the cabin and announced,

'Hello, I'm Dawn.'

Barbara quickly overcame her slight prejudice against the name, which for some reason struck her as a little gimmicky, but she was honest enough to realize that people who liked the name 'Dawn' probably regarded 'Barbara' as plain and old-hat. Fortunately, she liked the look of her temporary companion and was pleased to find that they quickly struck up a short-term acquaintance as though they had known one another for months. This said a good deal for Dawn's friendly manner and Barbara's new-found confidence. In fact, Barbara's first real experience of being quickly friendly with strangers had been in a hostel. There, however, everybody had had at least one interest in common.

'You on holiday?' Dawn asked.

'Yes,' Barbara replied. 'Just a quick fortnight's tour of Scandinavia. I've never been there before.'

'All on your ownio?'

'Yes.'

Dawn looked so surprised that Barbara told her her curious

story, with the usual down grading of the legacy at the end of it all.

'Some people,' said Dawn, 'have all the luck. I had to save up for months for my holiday.'

Barbara felt quite sorry that she had more or less been forced into revealing her good luck. She never liked showing off, still less if it disappointed anyone, ever.

'You alone too?' she asked.

'Not really. I am travelling alone, but I'm going to meet my fiancé and work in Denmark all summer, as I did last year.'

'An English firm or something?'

'No, I am working in a hotel. That's my line.'

'But,' Barbara commented, 'what about the language?'

'I can get by in Danish.' Dawn smiled.

'But what an odd – I mean, what an unusual language to know.'

'I was there for six months last year and the year before that, and I picked it up as I went along.'

Barbara felt, to her surprise, a pang of envy. She reckoned to be good at languages, but she had to study the grammar to see how a language worked. She could not begin to pick up a language by just listening.

'Well – er – congratulations,' said Barbara sincerely. 'I mean on the engagement and on learning the language so quickly.'

'I did have a sleeping dictionary.'

Barbara was genuinely puzzled for a moment. She had never heard the phrase before; then she saw the point.

'Oh yes,' she said. 'I suppose so.'

'You look a bit shocked,' said Dawn, clearly not minding in the least.

'Did I? I didn't mean to – really.'

'That's OK . . . but, but . . . '

Dawn broke off and seemed very undecided as to whether or not to continue. Barbara was surprised. She did not look the kind of girl who would ever hesitate about anything.

'Well,' Dawn resumed, 'I shall not be seeing you again after tomorrow, so I'll tell you about something I'm a bit worried about.'

'Not if you don't want to.'

'Yes. I do want to, actually – but,' and she smiled, 'you don't look like a Catholic priest.'

'A Catholic priest?' Barbara echoed.

'For my confessional.'

'Oh, I see.'

'Well, I'm a bit ashamed of myself, really. You see, I've picked up a boyfriend in England too.'

'Yes?'

'Well, what do you think?'

Barbara hesitated.

'I'm sorry to be dense, but surely if the Danish boy is your fiancé, you'll have to stick with him unless you break it off.'

'Well,' Dawn explained, 'he's only my fiancé in a manner of speaking.'

This was getting a bit beyond Barbara. To her, a fiancé was a fiancé.

'Well,' said Barbara – she was beginning to catch Dawn's habit of beginning every sentence with that word – 'Are you actually in love with one of them?'

'No problem there; with Erik, I mean my fiancé in Denmark.'

'Well then.'

That was a different kind of 'Well'.

Dawn looked very taken aback by that cryptic comment and did not speak for a full minute. Luckily for her, Barbara was a patient person and she did not try to break the long silence.

At last, Dawn smiled. She was good at smiling.

'Have you read about the Samaritans?' she asked. 'They say that they make people answer their own questions. Thank you, I'll dispose of Frank.'

Barbara was not used to acting as a confessor and felt a little overwhelmed by the responsibility of it.

'I'm not really the best sort of person to ask about that sort of thing,' she said humbly.

'Not to worry about that,' said Dawn happily. 'I've got the answer I really wanted. I'll write to Frank tomorrow.'

Having in this unprecedented way done her good turn for the day, Barbara began to enjoy the voyage. Never before had she set off on so long a sea-trip. Luckily, the sea was so slight that the journey was not marred by sea-sickness. After the sun had set, she went back on deck and was surprised by the pitch darkness. She was not at all used to sea-travel and the English Channel had been so full of lights at night. Here, in the North Sea, it seemed that her ship was quite alone in the ocean. This feeling was all the stronger because she was standing right at the stern of the boat, seeing almost nothing but a little phosphorescence in the waves as the ship churned up its wake. It felt quite sinister and Barbara almost rushed back into one of the lounges to gain reassurance from the bright lights and crowds of people.

The following morning, after an excellent night's sleep, Barbara and Dawn went into breakfast together. It seemed very odd to hear Dawn ordering breakfast in fluent Danish; even the waiter looked somewhat surprised. There are not many English people who speak any Scandinavian language, and Danish is said to be particularly difficult. As they approached the Danish coast, the ship reduced speed and threaded her way through a small archipelago. It was all most attractive, but the tops of the masts of a ship protruding out of the water at one point showed that rocks could be ignored at one's peril.

When they had landed at Esbjerg, they found that a very attractive boat-train was waiting on the quay. It seemed quite odd to Barbara that the number on the back of her reserved seat corresponded with the number on the ticket, which had been issued many days earlier and in a distant land. There was, of course, no earthly reason why it should not, but somehow, in an unknown foreign country, it seemed more than usually efficient that it should. Xenophobia in disguise perhaps?

It was a very comfortable train, and it crossed from Jutland to the Island of Fyn by bridge. However, to get from there to another island, Zealand, it had to travel on board ship. The train slowly approached the harbour and was then divided into two halves, which were carefully shunted on board. As the train clonked on to the ferry all that could be seen by the passengers was the inside of the hull of the ship – a very dull view.

However, when the train had been fully embarked, the passengers were allowed out of the coaches, so Barbara joined the long line of people swarming up the stairs on board the ship, which was so well appointed that it amounted almost to a cruise liner, complete with cafés and restaurants, lounges and promenade decks. It felt like a dream. The ferry was larger than the ship which had travelled from England to Denmark. It seemed very strange, towards the end of the ferry journey, to go down stairway after stairway following signs to 'Platform 2', actually on board a ship. No wonder the vessel was so large.

The remainder of the journey to Copenhagen seemed almost uninteresting by comparison, although Barbara was delighted by the neat green fields teeming with black and white cattle. Denmark was a charming little country. On reaching the Danish capital, Barbara was pleased to be able to have a little walk to the taxi rank; she seemed to have been travelling for ages. The taxi took her to her hotel, where she found a nice spacious bedroom, complete with private shower, which, after so long a journey was more than usually welcome.

Much refreshed, Barbara asked at the reception desk how to reach the town centre, and she was advised to buy a little card for use on the buses during her stay. It was explained that she would have to put the card into a machine immediately on boarding a bus. She bought such a card and was amused to find that, once the card had been inserted into the machine, there was a loud clonking noise as the machine cut off and swallowed a section of the card and stamped the date and time on part of the card which she retained. It struck Barbara that part of the fun of any foreign holiday was that different things happened, not necessarily interesting things in themselves but interesting because they were new and unexpected. Barbara was particularly pleased to have this card because it meant that she did not have to know where to get off. When she saw the Central Station, she left the bus – only railway companies seemed to use the curious word 'alight' – and went into the first restaurant she saw.

After a meal, which was especially welcome because she had eaten very little since breakfast, she made her way into the Tivoli Gardens, a large pleasure park, and she really enjoyed the festive atmosphere, although she did regret being alone. How much more fun it would have been with Peter, or even

Brenda. The evening ended with a dramatic and colourful display of fireworks showering down the sky. Barbara had always been attracted by colours and by the names of colours. An unimaginative vicar had once done her considerable harm, as a child, by explaining in detail why, in his silly opinion, Joseph's 'coat of many colours' was probably white. She had soon discarded that drab idea and, as she looked at the rockets bursting above her head, she again recalled that lovely long list of all the colours of the rainbow as she had done by a waterfall in the Lake District. How long ago that was. She remembered that her interest in the colours of the spectrum had first been aroused by a glorious picture in an encyclopaedia at her childhood home, a picture that would remain with her all her life. She glanced again at the sky as the rockets died away and returned rapidly to her hotel and was soon fast asleep.

When, the following morning, she had at last persuaded herself to leave the surprising sumptuousness of the bedroom, she went down to breakfast. The enormous display of cold meats and cheeses, buffet-style, looked very strange and foreign. It was Sunday and, partly to please Edna the next time she wrote to her, Barbara decided to go to the Anglican Church. She found her way there, through an attractive park, with no difficulty. As she walked through the park, she saw, in the distance, a surprisingly English-looking church. She already knew, from the guide-book, that it was Church of England but she had not expected it to look so very English. She had forgotten that the late Queen Alexandra was a Dane, and it was she who had arranged for so very English a church to be built in Copenhagen.

All visitors to the Danish capital go to see the Mermaid, but Barbara was surprised to find that, in Danish, she was called *En lille Hafenfru* which she correctly guessed meant 'The little Harbour-girl' which somehow sounded more pathetic. Barbara knew the Hans Andersen story; the little girl still gazes so sadly towards the sea. The statue was not very easy to find; the Danes, much to Barbara's delight, clearly regard the Mermaid as their own little *hafenfru* and not as a tourist attraction. The only notices were small and in Danish.

The following day, Barbara left Copenhagen with some reluctance and went, by train, to Gothenburg. The train again travelled by ferry, but for a short distance this time. Barbara went out that evening to explore the town. It was a most palatial place; indeed, for Barbara, much too palatial. The enormously wide streets and the affluent looking houses made her wonder whether she had landed on Mars by mistake. As her footsteps echoed in the surrounding silence, it seemed to her, until she reached the more central parts of the city, that she was the only living person. She was very glad to discover that the town centre seemed much more like a place which was actually inhabited by human beings. After a meal, she decided to go back to the hotel by a different route; she had had enough of grand but sepulchral silence. The route she took this time went through a much less rich area and she was surprised by the large number of cyclists she met in the smaller streets. Often, however, they had their own cycle tracks and, where these crossed a street, they had their own miniature traffic lights, like a toy for the child who has everything.

Barbara became so fascinated by this cycling complex that she suddenly realized that she was lost. She came to a railway and decided rapidly that, as she had not crossed it already, she had better turn round. She wandered past a huge tram depôt and was becoming quite worried, when she suddenly saw something familiar. With a sigh partly of relief and partly, oddly enough of disappointment that the strange dream-like experience had come to an end, she retraced her steps to the hotel.

The following morning, she set off to fulfil the second part of the clue. She went to a little quay on the picturesque canal and bought a ticket for a trip round the harbour on a small flat-bottomed boat. It left the jetty and threaded its way slowly along the canal, indeed almost along the streets – they were so close to the water. At one point – and this was the event which she had been eagerly awaiting – the guide said, in three languages,

'We are now coming to the Cheese-cutter Bridge. It is aptly so-called and you are advised to sit on the planking of the deck to avoid decapitation.'

Barbara was, by now, beginning to get used to the BBC type English that so many Scandinavians spoke.

'Are the British,' Barbara wondered 'a much more litigious

nation than the Swedes?'

Certainly, no British boat would be allowed to take passengers under so low a bridge, and, even if it were, the warning would be given much more definitely and frighteningly than the casual sounding words of the guide, more or less implying that if you particularly wanted to have your head knocked off that was your business and none of hers.

Everybody kept their heads, both literally and metaphorically, and the boat sailed on for its trip round the harbour before returning to the town centre by a much less dangerous route.

Barbara did not stay long in Gothenberg; there was something rather too materialistic and successful about it for her taste. Also, for the first time since her new life had started, she felt frequently very lonely. Nobody knew who she was or could, it seemed, have cared less about her. After the much more friendly atmosphere of Copenhagen, it felt very strange. Nobody was actually rude to her, but the usual indifference of a large city, which for some reason seemed magnified here, was beginning to get her down. Indeed, she was not sorry when, after a couple of days, she continued her journey to Oslo, much cheered by a letter from Peter.

The very first evening that she was in Oslo, she found a most attractive floodlit square, called Studentenlund, complete with a very noisy and boisterous café-cum-bar, which, not surprisingly, was full of very happy and jolly students. Although she had Peter's letter in her handbag, Barbara was still feeling very lonely in the midst of all these chattering people and she was very glad when one girl student started talking to her, in charming but not totally correct English. She tried to explain to Barbara that the University of Oslo taught mainly 'Medicine and Juice', or at least that was what Barbara understood her to say. Completely baffled for a minute, she suddenly recalled that the Latin word 'jus' meant 'law'. That solved the riddle, but Barbara was just a little disappointed. Wouldn't it be interesting to have a degree, with honours in Orangeade and with Limejuice as a subsidiary subject!

For the few days of her stay in Oslo, Barbara not only wandered, with great interest round the city on foot or by one of the surprisingly dear trams, which were the only vehicles allowed, at walking pace, through a pedestrian precinct, but she also took a train to a little town called Drammen. Every time that the train stopped at a station, a voice through the intercom announced 'Dorer lookis' – at least that was what it sounded like. As that announcement was always followed by the doors closing, Barbara assumed that that was what it meant. She had a delightful small ramble from Drammen and was pleased and surprised to find a small café in the open-air, where she had coffee. She seemed to be the only customer, which did not altogether amaze her as the café seemed to be in the middle of nowhere.

The excursion that she most enjoyed was a two-hour boat-trip on the beautiful Oslo Fjord. It was a very interesting excursion and she was fascinated to see a large German passenger ship from Kiel sailing majestically along the fjord to Oslo Harbour. The guide, who was a typically blond Scandinavian girl, talked to each of the passengers personally, which made Barbara feel very much less alone.

She continued to go each evening to the Studentenlund and the atmosphere there was always so jolly that she could not feel excluded from the general air of happiness which pervaded it, although nobody else, except one girl who addressed her in Norwegian (presumably) actually spoke to her. Nevertheless, she was beginning to feel a little homesick again before the end of her visit and she was not particularly sorry when the time came for her to start on the long journey back to Copenhagen. The part that she most enjoyed was when the train ran along the shores of several beautiful lakes just past the Swedish frontier. Reaching Copenhagen late in the evening, Barbara was amazed to find how much she felt at home in that city. Less than a fortnight earlier, she had never even set foot in it. On the last day, she set off early in the morning for the boat-train to Esbjerg. It seemed very odd to be surrounded, after what had seemed to be a very long time, by so many English people.

The boat trip back was not quite so smooth and Barbara particularly disliked the feeling of going 'down, upstairs' which she experienced by going up a staircase on board while the bows of the ship dipped into a trough, a situation which her physics teacher might well have described as a 'perceptual discrepancy'. She wisely decided to retire early to her bunk, where she was not disturbed by a taciturn Swedish woman who shared her cabin. As Barbara admitted to herself, the silence and seeming unfriendliness may have been more apparent than real; she seemed to be one of the few Swedes who did not speak more than a few words of English.

The boat-train waiting at Harwich seemed, as always, remarkably small by comparison with foreign trains, and it was quite a joy to be surrounded by the cacophonous twang of Cockney voices at Liverpool Street.

For the first time since her adventures had begun, Barbara was not positively delighted to be back in her little flat. Its cosiness and privacy had always before been a welcome refuge. Her Scandinavian trip had, however, been so full of silence - nobody but Dawn and, to a lesser extent, one Norwegian student had talked to her - that she would have welcomed on this occasion someone to chat to in her flat. It struck her as odd that this last 'adventure' would have been the one that, some months ago, she would most have enjoyed, simply because of the fact that she was left alone - indeed virtually ignored - by strangers. She realized, with some pleasure how much she had changed.

Sitting over a pot of tea after her supper, Barbara was delighted to read the two letters which had been lying on her mat, one from Peter and one from Edna. Barbara felt a little ungrateful as she thouught that neither of them had the knack of writing very interesting letters but she was very glad to hear from them both and re-read each letter twice before going, for the first time for what had seemed a very long time, to her own little bed.

10

Quite unknown to Barbara at the time, a short interruption to her 'set' adventures was in store for her.

Juliet Roberts, a cousin of Barbara's, was feeling very unhappy. To her great consternation and distress, she was a voluntary patient in, of all things, a mental hospital. Juliet had been a very happy and outgoing girl to whom the very idea of a stay in a mental hospital would have been unthinkable just three months earlier. Indeed, in the unfeeling and unimaginative way in which people without experience of them tend to behave, she would probably have referred to them, incorrectly, as 'loony bins'. And now, here she was in one of them herself. She would never again use so unkind a description of them. Juliet was feeling, for the first time in her life, she was twenty-five years old, very lonely and friendless. Life seemed, quite suddenly, to hold nothing for her; for her, of all people, to whom life had been so full of seemingly endless attractions and joys. Everything now was dreary, stale and flat. Her sad outlook was not helped by the equally, at least, melancholy attitude of so many of her fellow-patients.

She felt that she desperately needed a friend who did not know what had actually happened to her. The friend could of course be told the bare facts, but she needed somebody who had not been around when it had all happened. She cast around in her mind for anyone who could fulfil this requirement. After racking her brains for hours, and indeed tossing restlessly in her bed until a nurse gave her a sedative, she suddenly thought of Barbara. Yes, Barbara, staid and unexcitable old Barbara would be the perfect answer to her search – if only she could and would. Without realizing that she was the only person left in the world who saw in the

Barbara she had known someone quite marvellous hidden so far below the surface that only she and great-uncle Tom had guessed the truth, Juliet decided to act on her belief. The late Mr Thomas Lindley would have been surprised and pleased.

The very next morning, Juliet put her idea to the psychiatrist, who promised to write to Barbara. And so it was that, on the very next day after her return from Denmark, Barbara found on her mat a neat typed envelope. Not expecting to read anything of particular interest, Barbara slit open the envelope quite casually. For the first time since receiving her first letter from James Garton, Barbara was in for a surprise.

Dear Miss Lindley,
I am writing to you on behalf of your cousin, Miss Juliet Roberts. I am sorry to inform you that she has undergone a severe mental breakdown and is now a voluntary patient at this hospital.

With my strong approval, she has given serious thought to the idea of contacting a friend who might help her to resume her normal life. She has given me your name. It is appreciated, of course, that you are no doubt fully occupied, and I am, therefore, reluctant to ask, on behalf of my patient, that you should do something entirely for her benefit, which may be of considerable, although temporary, inconvenience to you. If, however, you could see your way to giving some of your doubtless valuable time to your cousin in the hour of her need, I am convinced that the benefit which you would confer on her would be out of all proportion to the effort that I am requesting you to make. If, therefore, you are willing to do this, I shall be most obliged if you will telephone this hospital and ask to speak to me personally. I have mentioned the point to my secretary.

Yours very sincerely,

Alan Muirhead

Barbara was very moved by this appeal. She did not know her cousin at all well. They had seemed very different types, indeed, Barbara had always felt, on the rare occasions when they had met, that Juliet was a very happy jolly girl. What ever had happened to her? Barbara was not sorry that the word 'temporary' had been used in the letter. She was not quite so noble a person that she would have felt willing to undertake some kind of more or less perpetual obligation to her cousin. Apart from anything else, Barbara was still not exactly well off. In all probability, she would very soon become, in her opinion, positively rich, but not yet and, in any case, it was still not a certainty. However, she could easily afford both the time and the money for this unexpected errand of mercy.

While packing for the following day's journey, Barbara began to feel much happier. Of all the clues she had followed out so far, the least satisfying one had been the Scandinavian tour. She wondered why, and came to the conclusion that it was because she had not only been alone but because, in a way, it had been selfish; nobody else except, oddly enough, Dawn, had benefited at all.

The next morning, she went to Paddington Station and set off for a West Country town, where, after a quick lunch, she found her way to the hospital. She was ushered immediately into Dr Muirhead's room. As he had indicated in his letter, he had made certain that there would be no delays by his conscientious secretary, who was normally programmed to protect him from unexpected or unwelcome visitors.

'Thank you for coming so promptly, Miss Lindley,' he said. 'I am most grateful to you.'

'Fortunately,' said Barbara, 'I happened to be free when your letter came. I am not doing a regular job at the moment, but I am very much in the dark about all this.'

'I can enlighten you,' the doctor replied. 'I have Miss Roberts' permission to tell you everything that I consider necessary for you to know.

'Please.'

'My patient has recently had a most unfortunate experience. She had had an affair, lasting several months, with a man by whom she became pregnant. The man, whose name was Douglas – Miss Roberts refused to tell me his surname – then abruptly revealed to her, without any prior warning, that he was married, and he deserted your cousin. Miss Roberts had an abortion. The combined effect of these shocks resulted in a most severe breakdown and intense mental depression. She has been a patient here for about three weeks and there has been a considerable improvement, but whatever we can do does not supply her with a real friend. Could you possibly be that friend?'

'I would be glad to,' Barbara replied. 'I am very fond of Juliet and will do what I can. I do hope,' she added, 'that I don't sound at all luke-warm about all this, but Juliet and I have never been very close, so I have some doubt about my ability to succeed.'

'I think you will.' The doctor smiled. 'But there is, of course, another point. I don't doubt that you have a number of other things to do and this has been sprung on you at very short notice, has it not?'

Barbara smiled.

'In one way I have,' she said, 'and in another way, I haven't. Sorry to be rather cryptic but I don't want to take up your time pointlessly. I have been very tied-up for years but I have recently become much more free.'

'Don't worry,' said Dr Muirhead. 'All that I shall be most grateful if you will do is to spend a short time – even two days would be of great benefit but, to be honest, a week would be better – to be with your cousin when she leaves here.'

'Oh yes,' Barbara agreed. 'I can do much more than that. I could spend a whole fortnight with her.'

'That is very generous of you. May I take up your offer in bits, if that is possible?'

'I'm sorry?'

'Yes. I did express myself a shade obscurely. What I mean is that the ideal thing would be for you to spend a week with her in her own home and then to visit her just for a day once a week for the next few weeks. I don't mean,' he added hastily, 'that it has to be as mathematically exact as all that – a gap of two or three weeks would not matter. It is just that, if Miss Roberts can look forward to six or seven quick visits from you during the next two or three months, she will not feel your absence so much when you leave after your week's stay here. There is another point; if all this would be too expensive for you, I think I could help from a trust fund.'

'No, thank you,' Barbara replied. 'I shall not need financial help, but I appreciate the offer. As for the rest of it, there will be no problem about coming here. I do go away from time to time but never, normally, for more than a fortnight at a time.'

'I am very much obliged to you, Miss Lindley, for being so helpful.'

Barbara felt a little uncomfortable at all this praise.

'I am not really being so generous as all that,' she said. 'I was glad, to be honest, that you made it so clear that the help would be fairly temporary.'

'Of course you were. Nobody likes taking on an open-ended obligation.'

'True, I suppose,' Barbara agreed, 'but it seems a bit selfish, doesn't it?'

'We are all a bit selfish to one degree or another,' the doctor said, 'but what you have said to me is much more convincing than an offer of unlimited help, of which I would have been a little suspicious. Unctuous people who positively thank me for telling them how they could help usually go away to work out some way of backing off.'

'Thank you,' said Barbara, 'I have lots of faults, but I don't think that being unctuous is one of them.'

'There is another aspect of this,' Dr Muirhead continued. 'You have been very honest with me. I want you to be honest with Miss Roberts too.'

'How do you mean?'

'Give honest answers to her questions, don't smother her with loving-kindness. She has, basically, a strong character. All that I would be most grateful if you will do is to give her a friendly push in the right direction from time to time. The best analogy I can think of has to do with the old steam railways – or,' he smiled, 'are you not old enough to recall them well?'

'Oh yes, I can,' Barbara assured him.

'Well, in those days, it was the custom on some steep gradients to employ what were called banking engines. They waited at the lower end and then helped the main engine to get the train to the top, by pushing from the rear.'

Barbara was amused to recall James Garton's reference to his model railway. Perhaps Peter was concealing a similar passion?

'Yes, I see,' Barbara replied, 'but what exactly happened at the top of the hill?'

'The banking engine just stopped helping. It was not actually coupled to the train, you see.'

'It is a lovely metaphor,' said Barbara, 'I shall do my best to get Juliet's train to the top of the hill.'

'Not to get it there, Miss Lindley, but help her to get it there, will you?'

It was arranged that, in two days time, Barbara would call for Juliet and take her home by taxi.

Juliet lived in a charming little cottage with roses round the door, and Barbara was delighted when she saw it.

'What a lovely little house!'

'Yes. I like it too,' Juliet agreed. 'Welcome to "The Oaks".'

'My mother,' said Barbara, 'was brought up in a house called "The Elms" and when somebody pointed out to my grandmother that there were no elms in sight, she said "The only trees near here are planes and I could hardly call it 'The Planes' with three daughters of marriageable age".'

Juliet produced a wan smile.

'There are a few oaks around here, but I don't know about "marriageable".'

Barbara wondered whether she had said the wrong thing, but quickly decided that if she sieved everything before she said it, her conversation would become so stilted that it would be of less use to her cousin than ordinary talk, even if that included the occasional ill-advised remark.

Very soon they settled into a routine. Juliet seemed more than willing to do the cooking, but she was pleased to have help with the chores. After the first evening meal, Juliet said,

'I am really very grateful to you, Barbara. I could not have faced coming back to the cottage, all empty, all by myself.'

'I am sure you couldn't.'

'You see,' Juliet continued, 'I was so happy here, and now I am just all mixed up about it, and it is all going round and round in my silly head so I would like to talk to you about it – in bits and pieces probably. I shall not be very coherent at times, I expect.'

'Of course,' said Barbara, 'I shall probably not ask any questions, because I am not a particularly inquisitive sort of person, but that does not mean that I am not interested. Just talk about it, or don't talk about it, just as you feel at the time.'

They gazed for a while, in silence, at the flames flickering in the grate. Barbara correctly guessed that this helped more than speech. After a time, Juliet said,

'I wish that I hated Douglas, it would make things easier somehow. But, you see, I was very much in love with him and we were so happy for so long. I just can't believe that he is gone and never coming back again and that . . . he can't be trusted. I trusted him completely, you see.'

'I know you did.'

'I feel so very let down.'

'Of course you do.'

'How the Hell do you know?' Juliet almost shouted at her.

'You must credit me with a bit of imagination,' Barbara said. 'It is true that I don't know exactly how it feels because it has not happened to me, but I can sympathize with how it must feel, and if you don't think that I can do that properly, well just talk some more if you want to.'

'Sorry. You will just have to put up with me for a bit. I feel like hitting out sometimes. Douglas isn't here and you're the nearest target.'

'If it helps, hit away,' Barbara said.

'It is nice of you to be here and it is nice for me to have you here. Promise you won't go for a whole week, whatever I say.'

This reminded Barbara of the promises that she had extracted from Edna.

'Promise.'

'Thanks.'

After a lengthy silence, Juliet said, 'I feel so guilty about the abortion.'

Barbara could not think of a helpful reply.

'Do you think that it was dreadful of me?' Juliet asked.

'I don't know what to say,' Barbara admitted. 'I have never been in your shoes, so I think that I would be the wrong person to sit in judgement on it.'

'Well, thanks for not just saying soothing words, anyhow.'

'What exactly is a nervous breakdown?' Barbara asked.

She put the question on the spur of the moment with the idea of getting Juliet off the subject of the abortion. It seemed to her surprising that Juliet had not used a euphemism for that. It must have been a traumatic experience for her. Juliet did not answer immediately and Barbara began to wonder if she had said quite the wrong thing.

At last, Juliet said,

'It is nothing, just nothing. I had not thought about it before; but that is exactly what it really is. At its worst, I thought that I would do all sorts of terrible things but, actually, I did nothing. I couldn't do anything. I did not really want to do anything.'

Barbara was startled by the reply, but it made sense of a line in a hymn she had often sung at school assembly:

'Strength to those who else had halted'.

So that was what a nervous breakdown was – or at least the sort of breakdown that Juliet had had – a halt; not because there was an obstruction on the path ahead but because the path was so unattractive that you could not bring yourself to take another step forward on it.

'So now,' Barbara said, 'you are looking for something rather than nothing.'

'In a way, yes. I want to start living again, I suppose.'

'Congratulations,' said Barbara.

'I haven't done much to be congratulated about.'

'Oh yes you have, Juliet. You said that you wanted to start living again. That's great.'

'It is one step forward, two steps back sometimes, I'm afraid,' said Juliet. 'Everything keeps coming back to me.'

'I'm sure it does,' said Barbara, and, almost fearfully, waited for the come-back: 'How the Hell do you know?'; but, this time, it did not come.

Barbara resumed.

'If it wakes you in the night, wake me up too and we'll have a pot of tea together.'

'I may take you up on that.'

'It was a quite genuine suggestion.'

'Sure.'

They sat in silence for several minutes.

'I think I can get over Douglas, given time,' said Juliet at last, 'but it's this horrible guilt feeling about the abortion that keeps hitting me.'

'There is a thing I read once. It was written by, of all people, a medieval monk. It has helped me more than once, it may help you too: "Forwards look and let the backwards be".'

' "Forwards look and let the backwards be",' Juliet repeated, almost as though she was trying to learn it by heart.

'It will help, I think. People quote such silly things sometimes, don't they? But this one is – I can't think of the right word – it's sort of dignified.'

'Yes.'

'And a nervous breakdown is so undignified. Do you know that, at first, they would not even let me have a table-knife at meals!'

After a while Juliet added,

'One thing about a nervous breakdown is that it is thoroughly self-centred. Tell me about you.'

Barbara certainly had a story to tell and she told it with great enthusiasm, checking unobtrusively, at intervals, that Juliet really was interested. She stopped after a full half-hour.

'This seems to be going on for ever,' she said apologetically. 'Shall I stop now and we can have part two tomorrow.'

'No. Go on, please. It is taking me right out of myself.'

☆ ☆ ☆

Juliet worked in a bank. On the Wednesday, she went down to see the manager. She was very keen to restart work while Barbara was still around.

'It will be so nice to find you here when I get home,' she explained.

Juliet did a full day's work on the Thursday. Barbara was amused by the thought that she was herself getting practice for married life – if ever she had one – by preparing a nice meal for her cousin when she came home from work. It was all well worth while. When Juliet arrived home, she looked almost happy again.

'I'm back in the stream,' was how she put it.

The Friday evening was the last of that first visit.

'I don't know how I could have done without you,' Juliet said, 'but I think I can carry on now.'

'I'm so glad. But please ring me whenever you want to, in the middle of the night if you wish, and if I'm at home I'll answer. I can go to sleep again very easily.'

'Thanks.'

'I shall be away a fair bit, as you know. Will that be all right?'

'You are really asking me?' Juliet was surprised.

'Yes. I could postpone my travels if you want me to.'

'No, but thank you very much, Barbara,' said Juliet. 'I am really all right again now, but it was very nice of you to offer it. You must want to know what happens next.'

'Now that you are nearly your old self again,' Barbara said, 'I can say something that I could not very well say earlier. I'm just a bit worried in case you suddenly feel miserable again.'

'I expect I shall,' said Juliet in a surprisingly unconcerned tone, 'but I think I can deal with that now. I have a lot of friends. It's just that I didn't want too much sympathy to start with. I can take it now, and they do so mean to be helpful. You were the one I needed this week. And you came.'

11

Wondering what was next in store for her, Barbara set out with some trepidation to see James Garton. She was surprised to find that the more clues she successfully complied with, the more she was a little afraid that the next one would prove to be impossible. It was, oddly enough, not so much a wish to receive a large legacy as some kind of perfectionism; it would be disappointing to do so well at the beginning and then come unstuck towards the end.

She arrived at the office and produced a sheaf of tickets and receipts as evidence of her Scandinavian tour; they included a photograph of the Cheese-cutter Bridge – an interesting souvenir in itself. After he had examined them with interest, James produced an envelope on which was written the one word 'Barbara'. She looked a little surprised; it was one thing for James to address her, at her request, by her Christian name; it was quite another thing for him to write it on what was in a way a legal document without adding her surname. She had indeed become fond of adventures but some traces of her original primness remained to pop out and startle her from time to time. How odd! James was quick to notice her slight frown of annoyance and to guess its cause; he had a large number of older clients who did not wish their Christian names used in any circumstances.

'It is in your great-uncle's own handwriting,' he said, 'I understand that the envelope contains your next set of instructions.'

'Will they be difficult to solve?'

'I have no idea,' James gave an enigmatic smile.

'Oh.'

'It is a personal letter to you. This time, I have not seen it. May I suggest that you take it home to read?'

'Yes, please.'

Barbara was a little affected by the fact that the envelope and the letter inside it, she supposed, were in her great-uncle's own writing. She made her way home, feeling rather shaken by this posthumous letter even before she had read it. There had always before been some kind of anonymity about the clues that had reached her through the filter of a solicitors' office and in type, which is always somewhat impersonal.

Settled down at home with her usual pot of tea, she opened the letter.

My dear Barbara,

When you read this, you will have solved and followed successfully five of my clues (even if you needed help with the 'Merlota' one?). You will observe that I have said 'You will have' – not 'may have'. I feel sure that you have succeeded. I trust that you have enjoyed fulfilling an old man's dreams for him.

There are only two more of your labours to win the prize of the legacy.

On second thoughts, there are none. Having been in business all my life, I have become tired of people who do things for money and nothing but money.

It, therefore, really pleases me to state that this letter is part of my will and I hereby state – I am using words of this kind because, it seems that they are necessary to lawyers; I cannot think why – that the legacy is now yours without your fulfilling any further conditions. I have even had this letter witnessed in case that is necessary. You may well wonder why I referred to two further 'labours' as I have described them. Pray let me explain.

The two further clues (as I like to call them) were originally intended to be conditions that had to be solved and satisfied. I have now (quite suddenly but nonetheless definitely) decided otherwise. They do not HAVE to be satisfied. I am hoping that you will just want to do them partly for your own satisfaction and partly, although it may seem odd to you, to please me.

Of the two remaining 'clues' one will really be just another foreign holiday. I do hope that you enjoy them. Before that, however, I am asking you to do something rather more difficult. There will be no actual clue to solve, so this letter contains a misnomer, but never mind. The absence of a clue is because I want to make my request absolutely clear.

 I would like you to go for a week or so on one of the courses that are arranged in various parts of the country for outdoor activities. You will observe that I have deliberately used a vague description; I hope that it does not unduly worry my solicitor. On second thoughts, it cannot do that, because he does not have to have evidence of fulfilment on this occasion.

 May I be permitted to expand on what I have in mind? I have made this no doubt extraordinary will, because I wanted you to do things which, alas, I lacked the courage or clear incentive to do myself. On the other hand, it is so easy, particularly when one gets older, to be carried away, as they say, and to suppose that there are some very difficult things which anybody could do if he, or she, wanted to. I do not think that, in fact, this is true. I have always been ashamed of the fact that I am very unhappy on tall ladders. (I feel happier now that I have actually confessed to this for the first time in my life).

 You see, what I am asking you to do now is very difficult to define. I do NOT want you to do something of which you are so frightened that you probably could not do it. Please understand that. If, however, you attempt a course which you feel is going to be very difficult for you, I shall be satisfied even if you fail. I have often thought, when thinking back about my own humdrum existence, that the only way to fail is not to try; so 'failure', if it happens, will be, in a way, success. It has been a great joy to me, in my short remaining time on this earth, to plan these adventures for you. You have not let me down, whatever happens now, and I thank you.

 I sincerely hope that the idea of a treasure hunt has not seemed to you too childish a scheme. Perhaps I have entered into my second childhood.

 Thank you again, Barbara, for doing all that I have asked.

 In conclusion, may I wish you a long and happy life. My own has been long and successful, but not altogether happy.

 I have no children and have tried to project on to you, as it were, a route to happiness that I so sadly missed.

God bless you,

Your affectionate Uncle,

Tom.

Barbara folded the letter and cried.

After a while, she recovered and followed her usual practice, caused by years of living alone, of sitting and just thinking. Indeed, even before she had left home, with such great hopes, only recently fulfilled, her father, who had alas since died had once said to her,

'Barbara, are you just sitting or sitting and thinking?'

So, she could not attribute the practice solely to living by herself.

Her great-uncle's letter presented no real problems, and she decided that she would obey his wishes quite literally and resist the temptation to try to do something of which she was quite terrified in advance. Perhaps, she had inherited from Uncle Tom, although this seemed unlikely, her fear of heights. She was happy, normally, on mountains but not within inches of a great drop.

After she had ceased to think, she acted. She went to the library and looked up the Yellow Pages in a North Welsh telephone directory under 'Mountaineering' and found the entry: 'See Sports Clubs and Associations'. Like most of us, Barbara found this kind of cross-referencing somewhat offputting. However, she duly saw 'Sports Clubs and Associations' and then rang a possible number. She was lucky first time and asked for the brochure to be posted to her.

No sooner had she put the telephone down than the phone bell rang.

'Miss Barbara Lindley?' asked an unknown voice.

'Yes.'

'I believe that you took the part of the maid in "Zack".'

Very puzzled, Barbara admitted that she had. Whatever it was, this did not sound like an advertising call for double-glazing.

'You don't know me,' said the voice, 'so I will explain. Is this a convenient time to talk?'

Barbara was pleased by the question. So many people just ring and start talking at a time that suits them very well but without any enquiry as to whether it suits the person at the other end.

'Quite convenient, thank you,' said Barbara, still at a loss to guess what was going to be said next.

'I am the producer, or director if you prefer that, of an

amateur dramatic group in Ilford. We hope to produce "Zack" in five days time. We are in a bit of a fix – well that's an understatement. The girl who was playing the part of the maid has been taken ill and she can't possibly recover in time for the first night. You seem to be the only person who could help us out.'

Barbara was still startled and felt as though she was gasping for air. Her question, as she was the first to admit afterwards, was not highly intelligent.

'How?'

The voice at the other end was very tactful and did not sound annoyed by the question.

'If you could possibly take the part for us, we would be out of a really terrifying mess.'

'I am free to do it,' Barbara admitted, 'but I don't see how I could get back here from Ilford late at night.'

'Not to worry about that,' the producer said, obviously much relieved, 'we can ferry you back home. Does that mean that you will actually do it for us, please?'

'Of course,' Barbara said, rather to her own astonishment. Where were the reservations that, in the old days, she would certainly have added?

'Is there a rehearsal tonight?' she asked.

'Yes, if you can make it at such short notice. Do you want a car to pick you up?'

'Not to go there thanks, but, as I said, I shall certainly need one to take me home.'

'Of course. Thank you very, very much. It is sweet of you.'

'Don't thank me too early. I must spend the afternoon revising lines. What about costume?'

'We shall have to see whether Diane's costume will fit you,' the producer replied, 'but if not, I expect that one of the girls could alter it to fit you.'

'That's all right then.'

'It's very much all right. I am really very grateful.'

The producer then gave Barbara some very clear instructions about reaching the hall and with further obviously sincere thanks, he rang off.

After that bombshell, Barbara did not have time to think. It was not until much later that she realized what a rare and lovely thing it is to be indispensable. They really needed her at Ilford. Nobody else would do. There is such a thing as a seller's market, she knew, but she could not help wondering, in an amused way, how many conditions and demands she could have got away with; not that she wanted to, of course.

She went four times through her old lines, disappointed at first by unexpected blanks in her memory, and she had known them so well. She was much cheered at her fifth attempt. She then had lunch, because she had discovered the advantage of proper breaks; trying to do the lines six times, one after the other would have been muddling, but with a real break, then everything worked perfectly. She knew her lines again.

Feeling now quite happy that the part had come fully back to her, she set off in very good time for the unexpected rendezvous. She found the hall with no difficulty and, quite the reverse of what had happened when she had joined her own group, she found the producer and three of the cast already there, surprisingly early. They could not have been more pleased by her arrival if she had been the Queen; indeed, more so presumably, as there is no reason to suppose that Her Majesty knows the part of the maid in 'Zack'.

'Barbara Lindley?'

'Yes.'

'We are very pleased to see you. Welcome to honorary membership of the group. We have never had an honorary member before.'

The producer then introduced her to several members of the cast. It was a unique experience for Barbara to be accorded full honours as a VIP.

'Fortunately,' said the producer, 'we are very nicely ahead of schedule, so today and tomorrow we can afford to spend a lot of time on the parts of the play where the maid appears. As regards movements, we shall be glad to give you what amount to dictatorial powers,' he smiled and added, 'within reason. I do know that if you have been used to getting a particular cue from your left and you suddenly get it from your right, you can easily be badly thrown. You are doing so much for us that we all would be very willing to change any moves that confuse you.'

'Thank you,' said Barbara feeling, surprisingly perhaps, very humble about all this. 'Perhaps we could try it twice with your moves and if I get badly thrown out by any of them, I'll take up your offer.'

And so it was arranged.

On the second run through, Barbara needed only two prompts. For one of those, she simply apologized afterwards, but it was agreed that a change of move by one of the cast would clearly put right the other difficulty.

'It is actually a better move,' the producer agreed. 'I can easily see that a change of move by Alan leads on to your next line quite logically.'

Barbara could not imagine her own producer being willing to admit that somebody else's idea was better than his.

They then broke off for a few minutes for coffee. Barbara got the immediate impression that they really were a happy group; they got on so well with each other and, in offering her so many choices, they were really putting the play before themselves. She had obviously been unlucky with her own group and she began to see why Edna was so much enjoying being with hers.

'One thing that puzzles me,' said Barbara, 'is how you knew where to find me.'

'Simple when you know how, Miss Watson,' the producer replied. 'I telephoned the copyright people and asked for the phone number of the last group that did this play. Your producer told me your phone number and, fortunately, you were in when I rang.'

After coffee, they went through the bits in which Barbara was involved twice more, and at the fourth attempt, she was word-perfect.

Three evenings later after a dress-rehearsal the previous evening – it had exceptionally been postponed to accommodate Barbara – she discovered that courtesy afterwards; she would have waived the offer had she know of it – the first night arrived as first nights eventually do. Barbara had known this group less than five days, but already she felt completely at home with them – a strange difference from the isolation that she had always felt in her own group; a difference which was accounted for much more by the friendly nature of these people than by Barbara's own greatly increased confidence. The group lacked nothing in courtesy. On each of the first two evenings of the play, the producer went in front of the curtain and announced,

'Ladies and Gentlemen, As many of you will know already, Diane has had a very bad attack of flu and is still not yet fit to appear on stage – greatly to her disappointment. At the last minute, we have been lucky enough to find Miss Barbara Lindley who played Diane's rôle in her own group two or three months ago and has kindly consented to do the part again for us – and for you. The part of Sally will, therefore be played tonight by her and not by Diane as shown on your programmes. Thank you.'

The play went extremely well. They were such lovely people to act with, it made all the difference in the world. On the evening of the last performance, Diane, as Barbara had been informed in advance, managed to struggle to the theatre. At a very tactful moment when Diane was out of earshot, the producer said to Barbara,

'We have kept a seat for you in the front row. That will be all right because Diane does not know you when she sees you. Do you very much mind being ready to take over in the middle if necessary? Diane has not really recovered yet. She looked quite green when she arrived, but she is determined to do it.'

'Of course.'

It seemed very odd actually expecting to watch the whole play through as a member of the audience, or so she hoped, for the first time ever.

Barbara stayed in her seat during the interval as she had agreed to do in case she was suddenly needed. A member of the group brought her coffee and biscuits. They thought of everything, these people, realizing that Barbara could not go to get them for herself. She was not disturbed, and Diane carried on with enormous determination and considerable success.

The applause at the end was stunning. Barbara genuinely joined in the clapping. The performance had actually been very good indeed; the applause was not just an acknowledgement of a grand effort made by somebody who had not yet recovered from an illness. Barbara was not at all prepared for what happened next. After the cast had taken their final bow, the producer beckoned to her to appear on stage.

'Ladies and Gentlemen,' he said, 'may I introduce Barbara Lindley to you. You are the only one of our three audiences who don't know who she is. As most of you know, Diane has been very ill, but we were delighted to have her back with us to give such a spirited performance this evening. However, there would have been no performances at all if Barbara had not come to our rescue at very short notice indeed by agreeing to play the part of the maid in Diane's absence. We are all very, very grateful to her.'

More stunning applause.

Barbara had never felt before the emotions which she experienced then. She was delighted to find that her pleasure was solely due to her complete acceptance by the group and by the knowledge that her presence had been essential. Nobody else in the whole world had happened to be in a position to do what she had just done for them. She did not feel conceited at all. Indeed, she sincerely hoped that the tremendous and obviously sincere acclaim for her efforts had not diminished the applause given to anybody else. However, on second thoughts as her uncle might have said — he had used the phrase twice in his wonderful letter — it was obvious that these people were so completely welded into a group that they were all much more pleased that the play had gone so well than that any particular individual, except, strangely enough, herself, had contributed to it.

On her way to a crowded pub afterwards, it occurred to Barbara that the producer, in his charming little speech of thanks to her, had epitomized the fact of her complete acceptance by referring to her, first as 'Barbara Lindley' and then as 'Barbara' — the polite but distant prefix 'Miss' which he had used on the first night had, no doubt subconsciously, been omitted. In the pub, she was again thanked and congratulated by several people. One member of the cast, a girl called Anthea, came up to talk to her for a while. Barbara offered her a drink.

'A tomato juice, please.'

Barbara looked a little surprised. Did Anthea think it discourteous to ask her for a more expensive drink?

'I lost the toss,' said Anthea smiling.

'I'm sorry?'

'We are not exactly teetotallers here, you know, but Bob, the producer, is a fanatic when it comes to driving a car. He gets really cross if anybody drives who has had even quite a little to drink. I think he goes a bit far, but we do like and appreciate him very much, and as I'm driving you home, it's a tomato juice for me, please.'

'I'm sorry to do you down,' said Barbara. 'I am certainly very grateful for a lift to avoid that awkward journey at this time of night.'

'Honestly, it's a pleasure,' Anthea said. 'We really are very grateful to you and we really like you too, you know.'

12

The next morning, Barbara felt somewhat deflated. Being a temporary VIP had been fun and being for a short time indispensable had been deeply satisfying, but now it was all over and she was an ordinary person again, but not nearly such an ordinary person as she had been a few weeks earlier.

During breakfast, the postman called. Barbara was pleased to see on the mat a large envelope which, as she correctly guessed, came from the School of Outdoor Activities in North Wales. It was an attractive and detailed booklet, easy to understand. To start with, there was a real mountaineering course; well, 'no' to that. Barbara had come a long, long way in the past few months but mountaineering was still out. She then came to a fairly detailed description of a week which appealed to her;

GENERAL OUTDOORS COURSE.

There are many people who are fond, in a vague sort of way, of walking; but who would like to be better at understanding maps, happier with a compass and better equipped to deal with emergencies if they arise.

This course has been designed to train people to become reliable and safe in remote country far from roads. Part of the training involves a certain amount of endurance in difficult circumstances. On the other hand, the Principal of the School is well aware that those coming on this course will, in most cases, be on holiday and are unlikely to want so much endurance that they do not enjoy their time with us. The most difficult part of the course is programmed for the end of the week, when members are sent into fairly wild country – not as lone individuals but in small groups, usually consisting of four people. These groups are expected to stay away from the School for a period of about forty hours, which means that they must sleep in the open for one night. Windproof and waterproof sleeping-bags will be provided for this purpose.

Members will also be called upon to prepare their own meals from simple ingredients in primitive conditions. They will also be expected to cover a distance of about thirty miles in the allotted time.

If this course appeals to you, you are advised to book early, for two reasons: it is a popular course and, as the present Principal is retiring soon, it cannot be guaranteed that this particular course will be continued beyond the present season. Different people have different ideas and it may well be that the new Principal will change the nature of this somewhat unusual course next year.

Barbara liked the sound of this and immediately sent off a booking.

The following morning, she had a charming small surprise. There came through her letter-box a letter from the Ilford group enclosing a most attractive honorary membership card, signed by all the members of the group, a lovely souvenir. Barbara felt almost like framing it.

In preparing for the course, there was one thing which Barbara decided to do and one that she resolved not to do. The positive action was to go for a twenty mile walk – and she decided to ramble from Cranleigh to Horley. To make it a little more difficult, she decided to load up her rucksack with a large number of unnecessary things, just to add to the weight. She wondered what explanation she would give of her carrying such odd things as a heavy book on embroidery in the unlikely event of her being stopped by the police. There was absolutely no reason that she could think of why she should be stopped, but it amused her to think how her unlikely sounding explanation would be received.

In due course, she set off for her long walk and found it exhilarating and great fun. She compared the actual timings as she went along with those that she had estimated from the map. Walking to a time-table was very different from casual rambling, but each was enjoyable in a different way. Reaching Horley in the evening, she had a feeling of achievement. Certainly, when she took off her heavy rucksack in the station, she experienced, once again, the sensation of flying, so easy it was to walk without its weight. Travelling back to London, she felt rather superior to all the other passengers, none of whom, she supposed, had walked twenty miles that day.

The thing that she did not do this time was to go to the library. Whenever she had had an individual task to perform, that was what she had always done before, but it had been drummed into her by one of her schoolmistresses that it is often easier to teach an absolute beginner than somebody with a little knowledge, because there is nothing to unlearn. It said a lot for the schoolmistress concerned that Barbara remembered what she had said so many years afterwards and put it into practice. Barbara wondered whether anything which she ever said or did would affect anybody so long afterwards.

About three weeks later, she left Euston Station for North Wales with a pleasant feeling of expectancy. She was quite a seasoned traveller by now and she recalled, with slight amusement, mixed with nostalgia, the great feeling of adventure with which she had boarded another train from Euston so long ago to fulfil the very first of her clues.

She and one or two others on the same train were met, as arranged, by a tutor with a mini-bus. They drove along roads which gradually became narrower and steeper until they became little more than stony tracks. Barbara and the others were at last ushered into a large stone building and shown to their little cubicles.

'Everything is very simple here,' said the tutor, 'but you have got all the essentials.'

Barbara was delighted with her tiny room. It did indeed contain everything necessary in the smallest possible space without seeming impossibly overcrowded. There was even a bed-light over her bed; and Barbara always read in bed. Having washed and changed, she went down to the dining-room, or 'refectory' as it was rather quaintly called. She sat next to a much younger girl; indeed she noticed, on looking round, that, rather to her disappointment, she seemed to be comparatively old!

'Hello,' said her companion. 'I'm Linda.'

'And I'm Barbara.'

'I've just left school,' said Linda, 'and my people asked me what I wanted for a treat, so I chose this. They thought it was a funny sort of thing to choose, but I have always hankered after something like this.'

'As you can see,' Barbara smiled, 'I have not just left school, but, like you, I thought it might be fun.'

'Well, we'll meet a lot of other people here like us, I expect,' said Linda – and Barbara was quite pleased to be linked in that way with an eighteen year old.

'Most people would think we were mad,' Linda added.

'People do think that doing unusual things is mad,' Barbara agreed. Then she added, 'Perhaps that is what madness is in a way.'

'Who cares?' said Linda.

And Barbara envied her for having so confident a reaction; she herself still felt a little self-conscious when doing very unusual things.

Towards the end of the meal, the Principal clapped his hands and said,

'Welcome to the School. Some people think it odd that we call it a school but that is what it is. Will the people on the General Course, please follow me.'

Fifteen people, ten girls and five men, dutifully trooped out and followed the Principal to the common room.

'This is only just a short introductory session this evening. We start work tomorrow.' He paused and resumed. 'I know that this may be your holiday, but it is an active holiday, isn't it? The first three days of your course will consist of lectures followed by practical work, all in or near the School itself. We then come to the forty hour expedition and we end up with rather less strenuous things. Are there any questions?'

'Yes,' said one of the boys. 'Why don't we do the forty hour thing right at the end?'

'We used to,' was the reply, 'but occasionally, the weather turned out to be so appalling that the outing had to be curtailed or even, just once, cancelled. Everybody, I am glad to say,' he commented with a gentle smile, 'seemed to be disappointed rather than relieved. However, by changing the start to the fourth day, we have a day in hand to allow for postponement if necessary. We shall not postpone it unless really necessary. This is not supposed to be an easy course.'

Again, the gentle smile.

All this strongly reminded Barbara of the trekking week. They all either stayed on in the common room, chatting, or went for a little walk.

The first three days were very like being back in 'real' school, except that everybody had selected their course and were in a mood to enjoy it. The curriculum was very well-balanced between theory and practice. No sooner had they learnt how to understand a grid-reference, for example, than they had to go outside and find places so identified. The lessons also included some elementary instruction in first-aid and some very simple astronomy for walking at night. Barbara reflected that everybody rather enjoys feeling more learned than they really are. It seemed very grand to be learning about astronomy.

When the great day came for the forty hours expedition, Barbara found that there was only one man in her little group and two other girls. They set off immediately after a very early breakfast and were soon in a remote and mountainous area. They had been instructed to take it in turns to lead so that nobody would feel superior to anyone else. They were very lucky with the weather and made a good pace.

It was certainly a good way of getting to know people. The boy was called Brian and the other two girls were Iris and Caroline, who liked to be called by the rather charming abbreviation of 'Caro'. Barbara soon found that she liked and got on very well with two of the others; she reluctantly admitted to herself, however, that she really did not like Iris. In their briefing for the expedition, they had been told that part of their success or otherwise would depend on how well they got on together. For that reason and also because she liked to feel happy with other people, Barbara tried hard to like Iris. That was very difficult to do because Iris kept complaining. Her grumbles mainly took the form of saying how much she wished she had chosen some other kind of holiday – a querulous comment that she made at increasingly frequent intervals. In the middle of the afternoon, when it was Barbara's turn to lead, Brian and Caro speeded up, leaving Iris some yards behind.

'Barbara,' said Brian, 'Caro and I are getting really fed up with Iris. Do you think you could stop her complaining all the time?'

'Why me?'

'Well, I can't very well do it,' Brian answered, 'and Caro is younger than she is.'

'Full marks for tact,' thought Barbara. 'He could have said that I was older than she is.'

Aloud she said,

'I'm not very good at ticking people off.'

'It's a nasty job,' Caro admitted, 'but her everlasting grumbling is getting us down – you too, I expect.'

Barbara hesitated. Finally, with considerable reluctance, she said that she would try, whereupon Caro and Brian arranged 'accidentally on purpose' as Caro, not very originally put it, that Barbara would walk for a while with Iris as soon as the time came for Iris to lead.

Barbara really hated the idea of tackling her; but two people, apart from herself, would benefit if she succeeded. Also, if Iris proved quite impossible, well, Barbara had two allies and they would just have to put up with it.

Barbara summoned up all her courage and said to Iris,

'Aren't you enjoying this then?'

'No. Not much.'

'Well, why did you come?'

'I didn't think it would be as hard as this.'

'Didn't you? I thought the brochure was fairly clear.'

'Yes, well . . .'

'Then, what's biting you, Iris?'

'It was a toss-up whether I came on this or on a seaside holiday.'

'But you decided on this.'

'And now I wish I hadn't.'

Barbara was getting nowhere. She tried a different tack.

'Don't you like us then?'

'You're all right, I suppose,' Iris admitted grudgingly.

Barbara decided to be more definite and to risk sounding like an elderly aunt.

'Look, Iris,' she began, 'we are all finding this expedition a bit difficult, but, honestly, it doesn't help us if you keep complaining. Three of us are doing our best to enjoy this, even if you aren't. Could you try, just to please us?'

Iris did not reply immediately.

'All right.' She said at last, 'I'll try.'

'Thanks,' said Barbara, 'and I bet you'll find it better yourself, at least, I hope so. After all, we are stuck with each other for another thirty hours, so we may as well try to like each other.'

'Sorry,' said Iris, rather more cheerfully this time. 'I'll stop sulking, really.' And although she did not exactly become a ray of sunshine, she cheered up a lot.

The first day they managed to cover eighteen miles with heavy loads, which took a lot of doing, leaving only twelve for the second day. They had all agreed that the weather might not continue to be so good, so they might as well do much more than half on the first day. They had had to drop down to a little road in the afternoon and make for a remote phone box, to report back to the School that all was well. After that, they struck back into the hills again and carried on walking until about six in the evening. By then, they were all tired. They found a fairly sheltered hollow, near a little stream, for the night.

'After all that energy,' said Brian, pointing to the hollow, 'it's funny that it is called Pant something or other on the map.'

'The first thing after a wash,' said Caro, more practically, 'is a meal. Anybody fancy themselves as a cook?'

There was a silence, the usual sequel to a call for volunteers. Then, as though dredging it up from the depths, Iris, surprisingly, said,

'I am doing a course in hotel management and we have had some cookery lessons in it.'

'We'll leave it to you then,' said Barbara, concealing her astonishment but determined to get in quickly before somebody said the wrong thing, 'except that I will peel the potatoes.'

'And I'll do the washing up afterwards,' said Caro and Brian simultaneously.

An hour later, they all produced their plates and received a generous helping of stew. They all had the first mouthful and then Caro said, in surprised tones,

'But this is delicious.'

'That's only because you are hungry,' said Iris.

'Look, Iris,' said Caro, 'it is delicious, so don't run yourself down.'

'Nobody usually says that what I do is any good.'

'Then it is time that somebody did,' said Caro.

After a minute or two of silent appreciation of the excellent meal, Barbara said,

'I have a confession to make. I dodged the mountaineering course because I am afraid of heights.'

'I'm glad you said that,' Brian agreed. 'It sounds very unmasculine but so am I.'

'Did you see that abseiling?' Caro asked.

'That what?' Iris asked.

'The people coming down from a precipice, backwards.'

'I did,' said Barbara. 'I know they had a rope, of course, but I could never do that, rope or no rope.'

The conversation went on for over an hour; and everybody enjoyed it.

'I hope that nobody has a tape-recorder hidden away somewhere,' Brian said. 'I have never made so many confessions in my life.'

'With the weight of all we have had to carry,' said Caro, 'who on earth is likely to have a tape-recorder as well?'

It was really a very jolly evening and the talk was so interesting that they hardly noticed that they had done the washing-up at the same time.

Very tired by now, they all got out their sleeping bags and turned in for a night under the stars.

'I suppose this is uncomfortable,' said Caro, 'but I'm so tired that I haven't noticed.'

Neither had anybody else and no further sound was heard from any of them until seven in the morning.

By tacit consent, Iris made breakfast, which was much enjoyed, and the others washed up. The second day was not quite so energetic. They had done so much the day before that the remainder seemed easy by comparison. Indeed by that time, due more to the sincere praise of her supper than to Barbara's best powers of persuasion, even Iris really liked it.

A mile or so away from their temporary home – and it began to feel like home to them all for the first time – Iris said to Barbara,

'You know what? I'm glad I didn't have a seaside holiday

after all.'

They were the second of the four groups to get back.

'I'm pleased about that,' Barbara said to Brian.

'You are not disappointed that we didn't get back first?'

'Not at all,' Barbara replied. 'If I am good second-class, I am satisfied.'

'People like you,' said Brian, 'are very useful everywhere. There are probably more good leaders than good seconds-in-command.'

'Thank you,' said Barbara simply.

'It was meant to be a compliment,' Brian added, not quite sure whether Barbara meant what she said or was being sarcastic. He did not know her very well, and that she always meant what she said.

'I took it as that,' she replied. 'I meant "Thank you".'

They were quite looking forward to the last day when they had been promised something less energetic. Although it had been great fun to sleep in the open, they all appreciated the contrast of comfortable beds under a roof.

In the morning, they were taken out in mini-buses by a tutor unknown to them. They had no idea where they were going or for what purpose.

They were taken to the foot of a sheer rock about two hundred feet high. To Barbara's consternation, they were issued with crash-helmets. The new tutor said,

'We'll walk to the top of that and then abseil down.'

Barbara's heart sank into her boots and she felt the blood drain from her face. The thought of being lowered backwards down a cliff was terrifying. With her heart beating a hundred to the minute, she followed the others to the top, like one in a nightmare. The bottom seemed a very long way down! She watched three of the others standing on the edge with their backs to the drop and then disappearing from view.

Her turn came.

She moved to the edge – and then, suddenly, she just couldn't.

'No! No!' she said in a note of near hysteria.

'Very well,' said the tutor. He made no other comment.

Barbara watched miserably while, one by one, the others, even including Brian who had shared her fears of heights and, indeed, Iris lowered themselves over the rim.

This was her first real failure. She thought back over Uncle Tom's letter. He had allowed for this, she had not let him down. Nevertheless, when everybody else had gone over the top and the leader was about to dismantle the equipment, Barbara, much to her own surprise, heard herself say – perhaps overdramatically as she thought afterwards,

'I WILL do it.'

The leader just said, 'Good', showing neither astonishment nor admiration – perhaps he had met this before? Still trembling, Barbara forced herself to get into the harness and set off on the descent. Once started, like actually speaking on a stage, it did not seem too bad. Each second of watching the cliff face move upwards, as it seemed, was one second nearer the finish. She landed safely.

By then, the group had really become a group, and everybody else knew that the right thing to do was to behave just as they would have done if it just happened that it was Barbara's turn to go last. All was well. They really did have an easy afternoon. It consisted of a discussion session with the Principal about how they had enjoyed the course, or otherwise.

'Before I invite your comments,' the Principal began, 'let me say straight away that what happened this morning should never have happened. If this were an ordinary school and you were children, I might have felt obliged to pretend that I agreed with my tutor. However, it is not an ordinary school and you are not children. The tutor should have known that abseiling was not, and was certainly not intended to be, part of your course. His excuse was that you had had no warning of what was going to happen and that, therefore, you would not have had time to get nervous and worked up about it in advance. That is, of course, true. Fortunately, all worked out well. You all did it successfully and you are probably all glad now that it happened. On the other hand, you are not sworn to secrecy about this course and will no doubt tell your friends about it. Other people may be put off coming here in the future. With that in mind, I telephoned my successor at lunchtime. We see eye to eye about this. You have our word that what happened this morning will never happen again. A doctor who tells a child that something will not hurt and it does is never believed again by that child, is he? I hope and believe that you will trust this school in the future.'

13

One nice thing about getting back to the flat was finding her mail on the mat. This time, there was quite an accumulation and she was very pleased but, by now, scarcely surprised, to find another letter from Peter. It would probably, she admitted to herself, be rather dull, but it was always lovely to hear from him, particularly when it was a welcome home note.

This time, however, it was not dull at all.

My dear Barbara,

Welcome back from your stay in the mountains of Wales. I kept an eye on the weather forecasts and it seems that you were lucky. I suspect that my letters, so far, have not been exactly scintillating but there has not been a great deal to write about.

Now that there is something to write about. I am finding it very difficult – this is the seventh draft – because I should be very disappointed if nothing comes of my idea.

Obviously, living so far from you, I cannot just invite you out to dinner to hear all your interesting news. I may not be a good talker but I hope you will agree that I am a good listener, especially to your news.

At long last, I will come to the point. I can it seems, have several days off next month. I am very much hoping that, as we share an interest in walking, you might be willing to have a short walking holiday with me.

If you do like the idea, I shall be very, very glad and quite happy to leave the choice of area to you.

To give you time to think – I hate high-pressure salesmanship – I am putting this in writing first, but when you have had time to think about it, I shall ring you. I shall not leave it very long because, although I know the date of your return from Wales, you may for all I know be off immediately to Hindustan. If that happens, I shall just telephone each day until I do get an answer.

Yours,

Peter.

A real move at last. Barbara supposed that some young women might have felt that Peter's letter was too tentative for words, but she did not react in that way at all. She really appreciated his reluctance to ring her first and so, perhaps, to surprise her into an agreement. Peter's idea had really pleased Barbara and she began to consider which area to choose. In the end, she decided on the Yorkshire Dales. She did not yet know them at all and it would be lovely to explore them together; at least, she hoped so, but perhaps Peter did know them already and the fun of joint discovery would be missing. She had only two days to wait before her telephone rang.

'This is Peter.'
'And this, as you may have guessed, is Barbara.'
'Have you had my letter?'
'Yes.'
There then followed such a long pause that Barbara decided to put the poor fellow out of his misery.
'I think it is a splendid idea.'
'Marvellous.' Another pause. 'Where?'
'Do you know the Yorkshire Dales?'
'No.'
'Well, what do you think?'
'I said I would leave the choice entirely to you.'
'I know, but I don't want to dictate something.'
'Look Barbara,' said Peter. 'I am so delighted that you have agreed that if you had chosen the Isle of Dogs I would have been pleased.'
'Yes, well,' said Barbara, 'but we may as well choose a district that we both like to explore.'
'It would be great to explore the Dales together. Do you want to plan the details or do you want me to?'
'I would enjoy doing it,' Barbara replied, 'and as I am "retired" in a way - doesn't that sound odd? - I've got much

more time than you have.'

'Yes, that's true. Then I'll write to book. I want to do some of the work. I hope you don't mind if we make it something a bit less communal than hostels this time,' Peter said, 'but the er . . . er . . . main idea will be the same.'

'Yes, please,' said Barbara.

One of her virtues was an ability to pick up nuances very quickly and not just to ask 'What do you mean?' She had realized immediately that 'the main idea' was intended to mean separate bedrooms but that Peter was reluctant to spell that out more clearly. Barbara wondered how she would have reacted if the 'main idea' had been quite the reverse of that.

It was great fun planning the details. Her first move was to go to the London Map Centre for some maps and guidebooks. The centre is a curious shop. If all you want is a standard Ordnance Survey map, you are dealt with quickly and efficiently but if you want to be a VIP you have to buy a very large scale map.

Barbara travelled home and spread the maps out. After a lot of most enjoyable thought, she decided on two nights at Aysgarth, followed by short stays at two other villages in the area. It was lucky that the amount of money that she had received, in advance, from her great-uncle's estate made her free from having to watch every penny, so she rang Peter on three or four evenings. Sometimes, the phone was answered by Peter's mother, but she sounded very charming and very willing to put Barbara straight through to Peter. Obviously, she had no real option about it, but Barbara was glad that she sounded as though she was pleased to do it. It is surprising how you can pick up a lot about people on the telephone.

One evening, before her departure for Yorkshire, Barbara invited Edna for dinner, and it was great to see her again. Barbara had decided not to keep mentioning Peter, but she was in for a surprise. Edna had become friendly with one of her fellow actors, a boy called Donald. Barbara was delighted by this development. Edna had seemed so clearly destined for a lonely life that it was lovely that her taking up acting had produced this result. Barbara was very fond of Edna and had begun to wonder whether men were blind. Now that she had seen, at Ilford, how friendly an acting group could be, however, she was not very surprised, but still very pleased.

'If it hadn't been for your piece of luck, Barbara,' Edna said, 'this would never have happened to me. Isn't life odd?'

'Mm?'

'I am sure it only happened because of you,' Edna persisted. 'It was only when the prison doors opened for you that I realized that I was in a prison myself.'

Perhaps it was a drama group that was making Edna so picturesque in her metaphors.

'Yes,' said Barbara. 'It is odd. I wonder why people seem to need a stimulus from outside.'

'A lot of people don't, I think,' said Edna, 'but we did, you and I, didn't we, Barbie?'

The next day, Barbara rang James Garton to explain that she had done one of the two things mentioned in her great-uncle's letter but that she was now off on a jaunt of her own. She promised to visit his office in early October. Solving and fulfilling the clues was a bit like taking an Open University degree: she could clock up the credits as and when it was convenient for her, except that now the credits were voluntary and she was strictly entitled to claim the legacy straight away. Barbara did not quite know why she was being so casual about so large a sum of money, but, later, she was to be very glad that she had not rushed in to claim her prize.

14

The great day for the holiday came at last. Barbara had spent one week-end on a visit to Juliet and was pleased to see how well she was getting on.

Barbara really did think of setting out for a holiday with Peter as a 'great day'. She had had many adventures alone, or, at least, for which she had set out alone, but, this time, she would have a real companion and she was looking forward to it with joy. This would be an interesting contrast to her clues. With regard to them – especially at the beginning – she had not exactly looked forward to going. They were uncertainties, strange adventures bringing she knew not what, so that she would have to deal with them day by day, as they came. She had, almost deliberately, not anticipated them by thinking too much about them in advance. She might have been too frightened if she had. There was a lot, as it seemed to Barbara, in the song that John McCormack was fond of singing; 'Just for Today'. But this time, she could expect a really happy holiday. Didn't that make a lovely change. At that point in her meditations, Barbara thought at first that she was being disloyal to Uncle Tom; then she realized that, of course, she was not. She would not have met Peter except for the will. And so many other things simply would not have happened.

She was just manoeuvring herself, complete with large rucksack, out of her flat when she met the postman, an elderly man getting on for retirement, who seemed invariably cheerful,

'Off again?' he asked jovially.

'Yes. Yorkshire, this time.'

That postman had been delivering her mail ever since she had moved into the flat. It was he indeed who had put through her letter-box the momentous first letter from James Garton.

Barbara regarded him normally as the bringer of good news and thought that it would be mean not to satisfy his natural curiosity about her peculiar comings and goings in recent months.

'Yes. I have been away a lot, haven't I.?' she admitted. 'Well, you see, an uncle of mine left me a bit of money in his will, so I can do a lot of travelling for a while.'

It was typical of Barbara that she had added 'for a while'. She still tended to keep her options open. True, by now, she had 'earned' her legacy, but years and years of thinking that nothing interesting would ever come her way had made an impression that was still not quite eradicated. In any case, she did not propose to live the rest of her life without doing any work, and she was glad that her recent experiences had so much broadened her horizons that, by now, she was sure that she could get a much more interesting job if she wanted one. It seemed rather unfair.

'I hope you enjoy it, miss,' said the postman.

Barbara felt so happy that even if it had not been such a bright and sunny day, she would have enjoyed her urban walk to the station. She arrived at King's Cross in very good time for the train and had a leisurely cup of coffee before going on to the platform. Unlike most people, Barbara actually enjoyed waiting for a while when she was looking forward to what was going to happen next. The waiting seemed to enhance the subsequent event. Even British Rail coffee, which, although dear is, to be fair to it, good, seemed like nectar to her then.

Barbara liked the atmosphere of King's Cross station; it had neither the modernity of Euston nor the confusion of Liverpool Street. It did have an attractive simplicity which she liked very much. She went on board the train and settled down in a corner seat. Nobody was actually with her, but she was not alone; Peter would be joining the train at Doncaster and travelling with her to Northallerton. The journey to Doncaster seemed to take a very long time, not because she was impatient but because she was so happy that she enjoyed every minute of it. She was able to do something that she was very fond of – read a light novel and look out of the window at frequent intervals. It was a lovely mixture. She could never understand why some people are bored on trains.

At Doncaster, Barbara went to the window to wave at Peter, who waved back and ran to the door. Neither of them was very demonstrative, but the happy smiles which they exchanged on meeting were proof enough of their delight. From Northallerton, they went by buses to Aysgarth. It was a delightful journey, and Barbara would have enjoyed it even by herself. Motorists and trains usually go more or less straight from place to place, not so these buses. They could not, it seemed, bear to miss out a single village within two miles of the main road. Every time that they scented one, they left the main road and made a bee-line for the village. Peter had booked three nights for them at what turned out to be a charming old stone cottage, a bit like a miniature version of the Outdoor School. Barbara's lovely little bedroom had exposed beams and leaded windows, giving on to a delightful view of the dale. The room itself was neat and colourful, with a most cosy looking single bed and a reading lamp.

In a few minutes, they were shown into a small dining-room, with a fire burning in the grate. A very pleasant meal was served in next to no time. As they sat enjoying a pot of tea afterwards, Peter said,

'I haven't felt so peaceful for years.'

'Neither have I,' Barbara agreed. 'Isn't it nice that we have nothing more to do tonight – except perhaps a little stroll if we feel like it.'

'We'd better have a stroll,' said Peter. 'I expect that we'll feel so tired the next two nights that we shall not feel like having one then.'

Barbara suggested going out fairly soon, because the light would begin to fail in about an hour. They wandered along the river bank to see the famous Falls and strolled back again.

They warmed themselves by the fire. They turned out the electric light and watched the flickering flames and the shadows that danced on the walls.

'Isn't it quiet,' said Barbara. 'Where I live, there is a plane droning overhead every few minutes.'

'It is pretty quiet where I live,' Peter replied. 'In fact, it is much too quiet. We are in a cul-de-sac.'

'Wasn't there a man some time ago,' said Barbara, 'Joad I think he was called, who kept saying "It depends on what you mean by quiet", or whatever?'

'Yes, I've heard about him too. My mother used to listen to him on the radio. Mind you, he sounds a bit pedantic to me. Anyway, what are you getting at?'

'Well,' Barbara replied, 'the quiet here is peaceful quiet.'

Peter did not reply at once.

'You mean,' he said at last, 'that you can have a quietness which is disquieting?'

'Yes.'

'You are quite right, Barbara. The quiet I have at home is not the right kind of quiet.'

Again he paused, and then added,

'As I told you at Spa, I live with my mother; just the two of us and somehow, nothing seems to happen – except at Spa and now.'

'Thank you,' said Barbara, and added, 'I know exactly what you mean. Before all these extraordinary things started happening to me, my flat seemed quiet in that dull way, despite the aircraft.'

'I feel,' said Peter, 'a bit frustrated at times, not in any specific way that I could neatly define, but generally. I can't explain it any better than that.'

'You don't have to. That is how I often felt before Uncle Tom started all these things happening.'

'It has to do with companionship, I think,' said Peter.

'I am sure it has,' Barbara agreed. 'I think there are probably a few people who actually like living alone, but lots and lots of people live all by themselves and they don't want to at all.'

'Yes. I don't exactly live alone, but I don't have a companion in the sense of somebody of my own age.'

'Well,' Barbara smiled, 'you have got one now.'

'Yes, thank you,' said Peter simply. 'I have not overlooked that for one single moment. It is just that I am keen that you should not think that I am in some way trying to commit you to something. I am really not trying to tie you down. I refuse to think beyond this holiday.'

It was fortunate for Peter that Barbara too was basically a serious kind of person and that she did not think that his last remarks were too ponderous or over-cautious. She had been over-cautious herself until so recently and realized exactly why Peter was moving ahead so slowly. Had she been here with Bob, the evening would no doubt have been more exciting, but not really anything like so enjoyable for her. As she had said once to Edna, she did not hanker after excitement, except perhaps very occasionally.

They were very lucky with the weather during the following two days. Both on the Tuesday and the Wednesday, they walked all morning and sat down at midday to enjoy their sandwiches and flasks of hot coffee on the hills, or 'tops' as the local people called them. By that time of day, it was warm enough for them to rest for well over an hour and enjoy the peace of the countryside, broken only by the occasional baaing of a sheep. Sheepdogs did not seem to bark. No signs of any habitation were visible, but there must have been a farmhouse hidden away in the dale.

'Convention is a funny thing,' Peter said, apropos of nothing. 'Just because I am a man, I have assumed that you would prefer me to do the map-reading and leading.'

'I don't mind in the least.'

'But do you actually like doing it yourself?'

'Well, yes, sometimes; but at other times I like being led.'

'Right,' said Peter. 'I don't particularly enjoy it. Shall we each lead on alternate days?'

And so it was agreed.

The cheerful fire and the attractive meals which awaited them when they got back to the village were even more welcome than they had been on the day of their arrival, particularly as they were able to have baths before the meal and so felt completely rested as they chatted in front of the fire until it was time to go to bed.

'We are luckier than Lamartine,' said Peter unexpectedly.

'Mm?'

'A French poet.'

'I do know that,' Barbara said, 'but how was he so unlucky?'

'He wrote a very beautiful poem about a lake,' Peter continued.

Barbara knew that too but forbore to interrupt twice.

'The poem included,' Peter continued, 'the lines:

> *Ainsi toujours poussés vers de nouveaux rivages,*
> *Dans la nuit éternelle, emportés sans retour,*
> *Ne pourrons-nous jamais dans l'océan des âges*
> *Jeter l'ancre un seul jour?'*

'Say it again slowly,' Barbara requested, 'and I'll see if I can translate it.'

He did so and then Barbara sat for a while writing.

'Will this do?

Moving, day after day, towards new horizons
Carried onward always into the eternal night,
Can we never in time's great ocean
Cast anchor for a single day?'

'That's good,' said Peter.
'Well,' said Barbara, 'we have – haven't we?'
They went on sitting and just gazing at the fire.
'Mind you, I don't altogether agree,' said Barbara.
'You don't agree about what?'
'I don't think that we are heading for an endless night.'
'Neither do I,' said Peter.

15

After their three days at Aysgarth, Barbara and Peter moved on to another village – in another dale.

'It might have been more satisfying if we had actually walked here from Aysgarth instead of travelling by bus, but it did not occur to me before we left home and I've got too much luggage now to walk with it all.'

'So have I this time,' said Barbara, 'but it's nice to have a few more things with me.'

'You have actually had a proper walking tour, haven't you? You told me about it at Spa.'

'Oh yes, by myself.'

'That was very brave of you.'

'Not really. Thugs usually seem to live in large towns. I was not very likely to be attacked. I was really walking, not hitch-hiking.'

'But you might have broken an ankle or something.'

'I wasn't in such a remote area as all that – not nearly so unpopulated as this one. There are usually a fair number of walkers about in the Lake District.'

'Anyway,' said Peter, 'I have never been on a walking tour and although I said all that about its being more satisfying, I suspect that I really meant that I am glad that we don't have to carry all that weight on our backs. It's funny how dishonest human beings can be about themselves, without knowing that they are doing it.'

Barbara did not quite know how to reply to Peter's self-criticism. Perhaps, in a way, she was stronger than Peter or, to be more humble about it, more used to walking. She certainly had had no difficulty when carrying a pretty heavily loaded framed rucksack in the Lakes. It would not have been very tactful of her to say that she had indeed found an actual walking tour very satisfying and indeed more fun than any other kind of holiday alone. It had given her a wonderful feeling of independence to be able to move with all her kit. It had also been lovely to see, ahead of her, an unknown village in which she had booked a meal and had a bed for the night.

'Women's clothes are not so heavy as men's,' she said, 'so I suppose it's easier for us to carry everything we need for a week or so.'

Peter realized that Barbara had worked quite hard at finding an excuse for him, and he resolved that, one day, he too would try an actual tour – with her, given any luck.

They were not so fortunate as they had been with the weather and their first day's walk from their new base was in very wet and windy conditions. However, they ploughed on quite cheerfully and, by contrast, they more than normally enjoyed their hot baths and a substantial meal at the end of the day. Sitting, after supper, in the light of a blazing fire, Barbara felt that never in her life before had she been quite so happy and contented.

'It's mainly the warmth after the cold and wet outside, I suppose,' she said, 'but I am really enjoying all this luxury after battling with the rain in the hills, aren't you?'

' "What do they know of harbours who toss not on the sea?" ' Peter quoted.

'Yes, but I enjoyed the "tossing" too. I really thought that I was going to be blown off the path at one corner.'

'I'm glad you were not.'

'So am I!'

'You are quite right, Barbara,' said Peter. 'Contrast is satisfying. If we had simply travelled here, we would not be enjoying the warmth in this room nearly so much.'

'I suppose there is something in the lunatic's remark that he liked banging his head against a wall because it felt so nice when he stopped.'

'True,' said Peter, 'but, as you said just now, we enjoyed our struggle with the elements. It was invigorating and, to use a phrase that is so overworked these days, it was a challenge.'

'The snag about a cliché' Barbara added, 'is that it has only become a cliché by being overused. I wish people would make certain that something really is a challenge before they call it that so glibly.'

'I hope I don't sound as though I were eighty,' Peter commented, 'but people will use such exaggerated words that it robs them of all meaning. The popular press is the worst offender, I think.'

'I hope that I don't sound like the popular press,' said Barbara, suppressing a yawn, 'but it's blowing half a gale outside, and much as I enjoyed contending with the wind and even the rain outside, I am very glad that I am not going out into it again tonight.'

'Yes,' Peter agreed, 'I would not do that walk again, without a full night's sleep, for five hundred pounds.'

There was a polite knock at the door and Mrs Butler, the proprietress of the guest-house, came in with two large and welcome mugs of cocoa. Half an hour later, feeling very pleasantly sleepy, although it was still only ten o'clock, they got up to go upstairs.

'The price has gone up,' said Peter.

'Mm?'

'It's a thousand pounds now. I wouldn't do that walk again now for a penny less than that.'

'I don't think I could,' said Barbara, 'whatever the reward.'

Tucked up cosily in her little bed, Barbara read for a while and then turned out the reading lamp. The wind was still howling and rain was being swept against the window panes. Although she was very tired, Barbara felt so happy that she resolved that she would not go straight to sleep. It was a delight simply to enjoy the feeling of being warm and confined, with nothing that had to be done for ten whole hours. How nice it was now not to be buffeted by the wind and the rain. Her bedroom was watertight and, apart from a window very slightly open, wind-proof. The bed became cosier and cosier and she fell fast asleep.

The following morning was delightfully bright and clear and the countryside had that 'washed' appearance that Barbara had first experienced in the Lake District. How different from the day before. Although neither of them was in the habit of eating a large breakfast, they both, on this occasion, really enjoyed ham and eggs, toast and marmalade and a pot of tea.

'This holiday is doing me good,' said Barbara. 'At home, I would no more think of tackling a breakfast this size than of flying over the moon.'

It was such a glorious day that Peter, whose turn it was to lead, decided that they would walk much further than he had originally planned. Not being so used to plotting a walk in wild country and estimating the time it would take as Barbara was by now, his enthusiasm outdid his energy. They thoroughly enjoyed the walk, but on the way home there was quite a marked silence for a while. Barbara, who was very sensitive to 'atmosphere', realized that it was not, this time, just a friendly happy silence, and she began to wonder whether she had in some mysterious way offended Peter. But although she racked her brains to recall anything that she had said or done in the past hour, she could think of nothing that seemed likely to have upset him. At last, she said,

'Is everything all right?'

'I am feeling very apologetic, that's all.'

'Apologetic! Whatever for?'

'I have badly underestimated the time it will take us to get back. It may be quite dark before we reach a proper road.'

'Oh. Is that all?' Barbara said, relieved.

'You don't mind?'

Peter felt so responsible for the error that he could hardly believe Barbara's lack of concern.

'Not at all. I thought you were unhappy about something, and I'm glad that that is all it is.'

'What a very charming thing to say. I was only unhappy because I thought you might be worried about being benighted or something.'

'I have a torch,' said Barbara.

'Good heavens. Did you expect this to happen?'

Barbara smiled.

'No. It is just that I am still quite absurdly cautious sometimes.'

'Cautious!' Peter echoed, 'after all your recent gallivants?'

'The operative word is "recent",' Barbara said. 'I was very lonely and cut off from most people for several years, remember. I have often had to overcome my caution in the last few months, and it can be quite an effort. I would probably have packed a torch on Midsummer's Day. Putting it in my rucksack was just a hangover from the past.'

'A very useful "hangover" on this occasion. I am very glad you did bring it.'

They walked on at a reasonably fast pace because they both wanted to be back on a proper track before dusk, if possible. It was typical of Barbara that she did not say, 'Show me where we are on the map now'.

'Well,' said Peter, 'I won't go on and on apologizing, but I hope that you will trust me to lead us again when it's my turn the day after tomorrow.'

'Of course,' Barbara replied and, after a pause she added, 'Have you ever seen a guide-dog off duty?'

'Not so far as I know,' Peter answered, 'but what has that got to do with anything?'

'A guide-dog has two different kinds of lead. If she is on one, she is responsible for the safety of her master. If she is on the other one, it means she is being led by a sighted person, and, then, she often does not even look when they are crossing a road.'

'Really?'

'Yes, really,' Barbara confirmed, 'and when you are leading, I don't even bother to think where we are.'

'Well,' said Peter, 'thank you, but I'll try not to make any more silly mistakes.'

Nevertheless, they were both very glad when they struck a wide clear track just before it became really dark. There was no moon to help them.

'There's a fairly new battery in my torch,' said Barbara, 'but I'll preserve it as far as I can. In any case, it is not pitch black and it is surprising how much you can see when your eyes have got used to the dark.'

They trudged on and, after a few minutes they were surprised to hear a rhythmical throbbing noise coming from a large stone barn in the fields.

'That's odd,' said Barbara.

'It's very odd,' Peter agreed.

'Could it be a milking shed?' Barbara asked.

'Not very likely,' Peter commented. 'This is almost entirely sheep country, we are still pretty high up here. I haven't seen a cow since soon after leaving the village, this morning.'

They walked on in silence for a while, and then Peter said,

'Barbara.'

And that was a little dramatic in itself, he did not normally begin sentences with her name.

'I am going to suggest something very peculiar and I hope you'll trust me.'

'I expect I shall.' Barbara smiled, and although Peter could not see the smile, he could hear it in her voice.

'I'll explain later, when we are back in civilization,' Peter continued, 'but if we hear anybody else coming along this track, I suggest that we keep very quiet and dodge behind the wall if there is a gap.'

'It sounds very mysterious,' said Barbara, 'but if you say so, sir.'

Peter was pleased with her use of the word 'sir'. Although it was meant to be jocular, it confirmed Barbara's willingness to trust him in very odd circumstances.

'Thanks,' he said laconically.

They had walked another half mile down the track, when Peter abruptly whispered,

'Listen.'

'Voices,' Barbara agreed.

'Yes. Look. There's a break in the wall just there. Let's go.'

Crouching down behind the dry-stone wall in the gathering dusk, Barbara felt, to her own considerable surprise, amused rather than frightened. She could not begin to imagine why Peter considered that this strange behaviour was necessary, but she did trust him and decided to enjoy this peculiar adventure. Uncle Tom had not thought of this one!

They did not have long to wait. Heavy footfalls got nearer and nearer. It felt surprisingly comforting to be so well concealed behind the wall. Two men were stumbling along the track carrying, with considerable difficulty, a fairly large and very heavy object.

'Why couldn't he bring the bloody thing up in the van?' one of the men asked.

'Didn't want any wheel tracks to be found,' his companion replied.

The footsteps passed and gradually receded into the distance. It reminded Barbara of a television film that she had seen, when the crew of a German U-boat sat in silence and fear as they heard the sound of a British destroyer going over them on the surface. As the sounds died away, they felt safe again.

After a good five minutes, Peter decided that it was safe to move, and on they went.

'Thanks very much,' Peter still used low tones. 'I think we had better go on being pretty quiet for a while in case there are any others. I'll explain all this later. I may be wrong but I don't think that we shall see anybody else.'

About twenty minutes later, they reached a small metalled road and saw the welcome lights of the village ahead of them.

'I'm enjoying this mystery,' Barbara said.

'Do you mean that you would actually rather that I postponed the explanation?'

'Just for a while, please. Perhaps I am being very childish, but this really is the strangest thing that has ever happened to me.'

'Very well,' said Peter, smiling, 'but it will have to be explained soon.'

Barbara was a little puzzled by that remark and was yet more surprised when Peter took, as it seemed to her, the wrong fork in the village.

'Where are we going?'

'You'll see soon.'

In a hundred yards or so, they came to a small cottage with the words 'West Yorkshire Police' over the entrance. Peter rang the bell and the door was opened by a young woman.

'Is the police officer at home, please?'

'Well,' said the girl, 'he is, but he's watching his favourite TV programme at the moment. Is it urgent?'

To Barbara's surprise, Peter answered with a very definite 'Yes'.

'Very well then,' said the girl, 'that's different.' She then called 'Jim'. The policeman appeared, looking none too pleased at the interruption.

'I am sorry to butt in like this,' said Peter, 'but I think I have found your forgers for you.'

'What!'

Peter described in detail what they had seen and heard on the track and he pointed out on the map the position of the stone barn.

'I hope you are right, sir,' said the policeman. 'I shall have to put through a phone call. Would you like to wait?'

'I would,' said Peter, 'but may I just run round the corner to our guest-house to stop them sending out a search party for us? We are already very late back.'

'Yes, sir. But please don't tell anybody what you have just told me.'

'Of course not.'

The young woman brought them a tray of tea. Coffee seemed to be regarded as a toffee-nosed drink in this part of Yorkshire. While they were drinking their very welcome tea, the policeman re-appeared and said enthusiastically,

'The Inspector thinks you are probably right, sir. We'll lay on a swoop straight away. Thank you very much indeed, sir, and goodnight.'

'But,' said Peter, 'we'd like to know if we are right. Can you ring us at Mrs Butler's – where we are staying – with any news?'

'The moment we know for sure,' said the policeman, adding, 'I don't think that Mrs Butler would thank me if I rang in the middle of the night, though.'

'True enough,' Peter agreed. 'The morning would be fine.'

They left the police cottage and made for the guest-house.

'Well!' said Barbara.

'I certainly hope that I am right. I shall feel all kinds of a fool if I'm not. I'm not very fond of melodrama.'

'I don't see that it would be very embarrassing even if you are not right,' Barbara said. 'The Inspector seems to have thought that your idea was a good one. Anyway, I expect that you are right. They would not have been worried about wheel-marks if they had been doing something honest. But how on earth did you know that the police were looking for a gang of forgers?'

'You remember that just before breakfast this morning I went out to get some pipe-tobacco?'

'Yes.'

'Well, I offered a five pound note in payment and the shopkeeper held it suspiciously up to the light and then refused to take it. He told me about the forgeries.'

'You didn't mention it to me at the time,' said Barbara.

'No. Frankly I found it embarrassing. I didn't like the fellow's manner. He sounded almost as though he was accusing me of having forged it myself.'

'I don't suppose for a moment that he thought that,' Barbara commented. 'I find it unpleasant myself if somebody refuses a coin that I had not noticed was foreign.'

They reached the guest-house and Mrs Butler thanked Peter for his earlier call.

'We were beginning to get a bit worried about you,' she said.

They had their baths and they were just finishing their evening meal when they heard the telephone ring.

'It's for you,' said Mrs Butler, with some surprise.

Peter answered it and all Barbara could hear was,

'Good . . . Not at all . . . with pleasure,' and then he rang off.

'They have caught them red-handed,' said Peter. 'Thanks again for trusting me. The way I behaved must have struck you as very weird at the time.'

'Well,' said Barbara, 'I either trust people or I don't. If I do, I don't question things.'

'Thank you, Barbara.'

'And what was the "with pleasure" all about?'

'They want us to look in at the police cottage tomorrow morning to be thanked officially.'

'And will they replace your forged note?'

'I doubt it,' said Peter, 'but it's been worth that, hasn't it?'

16

The following morning, Barbara and Peter set out for the police-cottage immediately after breakfast. They were greeted by the village policeman, who introduced them to the Inspector.

'This is just to thank you both very much indeed,' he said. 'We had been after that little gang for weeks, and we were beginning to despair of tracking them to their lair. Mind you,' he added with a wry smile, 'we rather resent being beaten by amateurs.'

'Sorry,' said Peter, 'but we were not trying to be clever. It just happened by chance.'

'You need not sound apologetic, sir,' said the Inspector. 'I was only joking. We are very glad to have that little lot under lock and key at last and we are most grateful to you both.'

'Shall we be needed as witnesses in the court case?' Barbara asked.

'Possibly. You will be given plenty of notice if so. The judge may want you to tell the court what you heard and saw. On the other hand there is plenty of other evidence against them, so you may well not be required at all.'

Feeling very virtuous, Barbara and Peter set off much later than usual for their walk.

'If I hadn't been such a poor map-reader, that would never have happened,' Peter said.

'It wasn't exactly poor map-reading,' Barbara assured him. 'It was just over-optimism. You thought that we could walk faster than we could.'

'Well, anyway, I do hope that we don't find today's walk an anti-climax. I don't suppose that we'll catch criminals every day.'

'Of course it won't be an anti-climax,' Barbara said. 'I just love this holiday.'

They walked on in silence for a minute.

'Talking of love,' said Peter, 'I expect you have guessed by now that I have fallen in love.'

Barbara was delighted.

'Thank you, Peter. Me too.'

'I shall miss you badly after the holiday,' Peter said. 'I want to ask you to marry me, please, but I'm not sure that you would want what that would mean. There's my mother, you see.'

'I don't see why that would matter,' said Barbara. 'You mean that we would be living with her?'

It took Peter several seconds to reply.

'You actually mean that you will marry me?'

He sounded quite surprised.

'Of course.'

And that was the signal for their first kiss.

'Mind you,' said Barbara with an enigmatic smile, 'there is certainly one condition, maybe two.'

Her tone of voice made it clear that Peter had nothing to worry about on that score.

'And they are?'

'Well, the first is that you must like my friend Edna.'

'What a charming provision. I am sure I shall. And the second condition?'

'There may not be a second condition. I haven't decided yet.'

'And you are not even going to tell me what it may be?'

'No,' Barbara replied mysteriously. 'Dear Peter, I wasn't expecting a proposal, well, not today anyway, and I hadn't prepared a pretty speech.'

'I don't need one Barbara. Well, if you won't tell me the second condition, you won't,' and then Peter asked, sounding slightly alarmed, 'You are sure it is a condition I could fulfil?'

'Oh yes.'

'I can't understand what you see in me,' said Peter, quite seriously, 'and I do know that most people want to live alone, together, I mean – at the start of a marriage.'

'Look, Peter,' Barbara replied, 'I'm so very happy about this that I won't give the idea another thought, so neither need you. I'm sure your mother is very charming.'

'Well, thank you again. Thank you very much. I'm sure I'm not saying all the right things. I can't really believe my good fortune. But I would have liked to offer you a house of your own.'

'Please don't worry. You've made me very, very happy.'

'And I'm sure that you will like my mother. Could you come and see her fairly soon?'

'Yes, of course,' said Barbara, and then she added in a different tone, 'And then there's mine.'

'I am so up in the air that you have said "Yes",' said Peter, 'or perhaps I should say "conditionally yes" that I am not being so bright and intelligent as I usually am, but what did your last cryptic pronouncement mean?'

'Sorry if I was being rather unintelligible. I meant that I ought to introduce you to my mother.'

'Naturally.'

'I am afraid that you may not like her very much.'

'I'm sure I shall.'

'Peter,' said Barbara almost severely, 'now that we are engaged, I don't think that we need ever be merely polite to each other again. Do you agree?'

'If by "merely polite" you mean insincere, then I agree.'

'Well, in that case, start by realizing that you may not like my mother. Shall I talk a bit about her?'

'Do.'

'I am rather ashamed of me.' Barbara began. 'I think I love her, but to be honest, I don't really like her very much. I did love my father, but he was in his fifties when he died. Mother is, I think much too serious and has such fixed ideas. You see, she never really recovered from my sister's death. I was the only one she had left and she became so over-protective that I resented it.'

'Of course, I understand.'

'I am sure you are doing your best, but I have only recently realized how much I felt that my mother frustrated me. Dash it, you must have noticed how – what's the word? – undemonstrative I am.'

'You!' said Peter, 'apologizing to me for being undemonstrative! What about me! Perhaps that is why we have got on so well together. It has been a real handicap to me that I have been awkward with girls.'

'But,' Barbara reminded him, 'you positively picked me up at Spa!'

Peter was pleased.

'Yes, I did, didn't I? But you have no idea what an effort that was. I had never done anything like it before.'

'It hadn't happened to me before either,' said Barbara, 'I didn't know how to respond.'

'That made two of us,' Peter commented, 'but it has led to the best of all possible results.'

And he kissed her again.

'We mustn't get carried away,' said Barbara, smiling. 'I am supposed to be leading this walk. How can I possibly read the map properly when you get between it and me?'

Peter laughed.

'Sorry,' he said, not meaning it at all. 'Lead on.'

'Right,' said Barbara a couple of minutes later. 'End of map-reading for a while. This should be a pretty straightforward path for the next couple of miles.'

'What I have nobly not been saying while you were busy with the map,' Peter said, 'is that engagement rings don't grow on stone walls. I am afraid that you will have to wait for that until the end of the holiday.'

'I am so happy just now, Peter,' Barbara answered, 'that I hadn't even given a thought to a ring, but, thanks, it will be very nice to have one later.'

'The other thing that was going on in my mind when I was forbidden to speak to you,' Peter smiled, 'is that I expect you would like to finish this treasure hunt of yours as soon as possible. I shall have to put up with not seeing you for a fortnight or so.'

'You think that I am very concerned about the legacy?'

'I don't think anything of the kind, but one of the things I do know about you is that you like to finish what you have started.'

'That's true, I do.'

'Any idea how much longer it will take?'

'There is only one more clue to do, so it's only a question of how quickly I start on that. I could have been doing it now.'

'And do you wish you had?'

'Of course not. I only said it to tease you. But isn't it funny that even this lovely, lovely thing is all due to Uncle Tom?'

'Yes, we would never have met in Spa otherwise.'

'But it is not just that,' said Barbara, musingly. 'You would not have looked at me twice a few months ago even if we had both been at Spa at the same time.'

Peter made a polite protest.

'Don't be just polite to me ever again,' said Barbara, but her smile robbed the remark of any criticism. 'I know that until all this happened, I was a dull sort of companion, and now I am not.'

'I can't believe that you were ever dull, Barbara,' said Peter, 'and I am not being "merely polite".'

'I don't believe that I was – inside, but, honestly, no man had ever taken me out more than twice, and I don't blame them.'

'Well, I do,' said Peter with obvious sincerity. 'I am just not going to agree that you could ever have been dull. Shy perhaps, but then, as this seems to be confession time, so was I, or whatever is the correct masculine word for that.'

They had a marvellous walk.

'Peter,' said Barbara as they neared the village on their way back, 'I have been surprised. I have really enjoyed today's walk, even more than usual.'

'I don't see what is so surprising about that. The weather has been good and the scenery great.'

'Yes, I know,' Barbara paused. 'It is just that I would have expected us to be so pleased at what has happened to me – I mean to us – that I would hardly have noticed the scenery.'

'I think it's because we are enjoying it together – really together, I mean.'

They settled down to an excellent meal by the fireside after their walk.

'I have been thinking some more,' said Peter. 'I had always thought that the first thing a man did on getting engaged was to buy a ring. I know you said that you were in no hurry about it, but if you would rather cancel tomorrow's walk and get a bus to Richmond or Darlington or somewhere we could, you know.'

'No, please,' said Barbara. 'I don't want to cancel a single walk on this lovely holiday. You can get me a ring on the way home.'

Then, after a pause, she added,

'Sorry if that sounds at all unfeminine or unromantic, but, you see, I had given up day-dreaming about marriage years and years ago.'

17

As things worked out, their visits to each other's mothers were very close together.

Barbara went, with some trepidation, to see Peter's mother. She felt very much as though she were on trial. There was obviously a clear and definite link between Peter and his mother so that she, Barbara, saw herself as an intruder, if not even perhaps as a rival. Barbara had become so used to thinking of Peter as Peter, that it had come almost as a surprise to her to recall that he had a surname too – Johns. She had, of course, needed to know it in order to write to him, and she needed to know it now in order to address his mother. Barbara was not the sort of girl who would have been happy to address her as Dorothy. Peter met her at Birmingham, New Street Station, and drove her to the attractive house some fifteen or so miles away, where he lived.

All Barbara's fears vanished when she met his mother. She was a little lady with silver hair and was obviously pleasant and welcoming. Barbara no longer felt on trial, but was accepted at once. That was a delightful beginning. There are not a great number of people, alas, who can make a stranger feel at home so quickly.

Barbara had planned to spend just the one night there. After dinner, they all sat and talked.

After a while, Mrs Johns said,

'I very rarely smoke these days but, Peter, will you get me some cigarettes from "The Lion"?'

Peter gave her a most charming smile.

'You would never have made an actress, mother.'

'Why not?'

'You are not convincing enough. All you want to do is to get me out of the way so that you can talk to Barbara alone, isn't

it?'
'Of course, dear.'
'Oh well, all right, then; but, whatever you do, don't show her photographs of me as a baby, will you?'
'Of course not. Nothing was further from my mind.'
With a good grace, Peter got ready to go out.
'How long do you want?' he asked.
'Half an hour will be ample.'
When Peter had gone, Mrs Johns gave Barbara one of her most charming smiles.
'I'm so pleased that I like you,' she said.
'Me too.'
'But I didn't have to make such clumsy arrangements to corner you just to tell you that. I want to hatch a plot.'
'A plot!'
Barbara wryly remembered her constant repetition of remarks made, so long ago, by James Garton at their first meeting, but she was still not good at reacting to surprising statements.
'Peter has been a marvellous son to me,' Mrs Johns continued, 'but, with the best will in the world, he goes too far sometimes. I've had a very happy life and, even now, I am not so disabled as all that. Peter thinks that you two have got to live here, but, you see, you haven't.'
'But I would be quite happy to live here, really.'
'But I would not like that,' said Mrs Johns, surprisingly.
Barbara felt hurt.
'But . . . but . . . I thought you said that you liked me.'
'I do, very, very much.'
'Well then?'
'I am old enough by now to have some fixed ideas,' said Mrs Johns, 'and nothing is likely to change them now. All married people should live in a house of their own if they possibly can, particularly at the beginning. It is no good arguing with me. I know.'
'But Peter has decided that we should live here.'
'You may have to do exactly what Peter wants. I don't.'
Barbara was bewildered.
'Well,' she said at last, 'what do you want me to do about it?'
'I simply want you to tell Peter that you want to live in your

own house.'

'Without telling him about this talk, you mean?'

It was the turn of Mrs Johns to hesitate.

'Would you prefer your own house?'

Barbara looked at her future mother-in-law and knew that an honest answer was required.

'Yes,' she said.

'Good. In that case, there is no problem. You want it and I want it and I am sure that, in the end, Peter would prefer it. So, you can bring me in as an ally, but it would be best, I think, if you make it quite clear first that that is what you would like. Will you do that for me?'

'I'll do it for all of us,' Barbara promised. 'I do like you. We won't live far away. I promise.'

The following week-end, it was Peter's turn to go to Kent to see Mrs Lindley for the first time. Not having a car, Barbara met Peter at Victoria Station and they travelled down together by rail. Peter did not particularly enjoy his visit to Kent because, just as Barbara had wrongly expected to feel under test by his mother, Peter rightly felt that he was being examined for faults.

Mrs Lindley did not have the tact or charm of manner displayed by Peter's mother and, instead of finding some pretext for sending Barbara away for half an hour, she insisted on making statements in her presence that made her positively squirm.

'You see, Mr Johns,' she said over dinner, 'Barbara is all I have left, so I am bound to be very concerned about a future husband for her.'

'Of course,' Peter said, feeling very uncomfortable, 'I shall do my best. I love her.'

Peter was aware that this sounded very stilted and perhaps even pedantic, but somehow Mrs Lindley's manner was so stern and serious that it produced pedantic and stilted replies. He simply could not feel accepted by her.

However, as the evening wore on, the ice melted considerably and Peter soon realized that, whatever else she was, Mrs Lindley was genuine in her concern for her daughter's happiness. He did his level best to reassure her. It was not the easiest possible task for him because he hated blowing his own trumpet, which was what he was being forced into doing.

After breakfast the next morning, he and Barbara travelled back to Victoria together.

'Are you in a hurry to get back home?' Barbara asked just as the train was running into the terminus.

'No, no. I can easily catch an evening train to Birmingham.'

'Good.'

'Shall we have lunch somewhere?' Peter suggested.

'That would be very nice.'

'You sound a little *distraite*,' Peter commented. 'It is not just lunch that you have in mind, is it?'

'No. Look, Peter, after lunch can we go for a little walk? I want to discuss something.'

Peter looked quite worried.

'Nothing serious?' he asked.

To his relief but also to his mystification, Barbara gave a secret smile.

'Quite the reverse,' she said.

After a very pleasant little lunch, during which they talked trivialities, they set off for St James's Park.

'You remember,' Barbara began, 'that I said that there might be a second condition to our marriage?'

'Yes, and you said that you were sure that I could comply with it.'

'I am now about to shock you,' said Barbara.

'I am sure you won't.'

'This is the third occasion,' said Barbara with mock severity, 'that I have had to ask you not to be just polite, although, on second thoughts I am not sure that contradicting me is the very thing that I shall always want.'

'You were saying,' said Peter tactfully, 'that you were going to shock me.'

'I know I said that, and it is quite true. But I am so unused to shocking people that I am finding it difficult to begin.'

'I'll just keep quiet, then,' Peter offered, 'and we'll stroll on until you feel like talking.'

'Thanks.'

A minute or so later, Barbara said, very earnestly,

'Peter, I am not exactly a young girl, and I am just a bit worried that I may not be a proper wife – please don't interrupt –. Could we, er, test that before we marry?'

Peter was very anxious not to embarrass Barbara or to make things even more difficult for her by spelling things out too precisely.

'You have put it very delicately,' he said.
'But you are still shocked, because it's me, I mean?'
'No. Oh, well, all right, yes.'
'I'm glad,' said Barbara.
Peter was speechless for a few seconds.
'You are glad?' he echoed at last, completely out of his depth. He had thought that he knew his fiancée.
'Now that I have broken the ice,' Barbara continued, 'let me explain some more, and please don't interrupt, however much you may want to.'
Peter nodded.
'It's funny, really,' Barbara resumed. 'Fifty years ago a prospective bride might have invited her fiancé for a quiet talk to confess to him that she was not a virgin. Things have changed so much that this amounts, in a way, to a confession that I am.'
She turned to Peter.
'And now,' she said, 'it's your turn.'
'You really don't have to do this, Barbara. I love you, don't you understand? And even if, and I don't suppose for a moment that it is likely, things didn't turn out well in bed, I would still want to marry you.'
'Darling Peter,' said Barbara, 'I know.'
'Well then?'
'I am very mixed up about all this,' Barbara admitted, 'but I have definitely made up my mind. I think I would have decided this way in any case, but there was a last straw.'
'What ever was that?'
'You must have noticed the way my mother put your bedroom at one end of the corridor and me at the other end – with her in the middle.'
'Well no,' said Peter, 'I hadn't noticed. It may have been just a coincidence.'
'Coincidence, fiddlesticks!' said Barbara with unusual vehemence.
'So you've got two reasons?'
'Yes. Yes, I have. I really want to see if everything is all right

before we marry and, as you have spotted pretty quickly, it will also be my last "break-out" from rules and regulations.'

'As you seem to have assumed,' said Peter, 'I have no objection.'

'Good heavens,' said Barbara, 'perhaps I should not have assumed that so readily – but I did.'

'We may as well get down to brass tacks. Knowing you as I do, I assume that you have some definite scheme in mind.'

'Oh, yes. I didn't just think in a vacuum. I really don't have any first-hand experience, as I have just told you, but the topic was talked about sometimes in the office and I gather that a motel is the answer.'

'Sorry if I seem extraordinarily dense on this,' said Peter, 'but why motels in particular and not just hotels?'

'The general idea seems to be,' Barbara replied, 'that a motel is more anonymous, and if we are going to do it anyway, we may as well enjoy it and benefit from other people's experience, don't you think?'

Certainly,' said Peter, 'I'll get out my list of hotels and motels and ring you later to discuss any details.'

'At least, it will be something new, and a surprising number of things have been new for me in the last six months.'

18

On the Friday evening three weeks later, Peter collected Barbara at her flat and they drove down to Sussex.

'I know,' said Peter with a smile, 'that this is an entirely new experience for you. And, strangely enough, I have never used a motel before.'

It felt very cosy in the car. It was a fairly cold evening and the headlights revealed green banks at the side of the road, making them look like fairyland. Peter drove into the car park of a motel and got out.

'Hang on here,' he said.

'If you can come back with a key and nobody in tow, it would simplify things, please.'

'I'll do my best.'

A few minutes later, he reappeared, alone.

'The chalets are over there,' he said. 'We can drive round. You don't have to pass the receptionist at all.'

'They must be used to this sort of thing,' Barbara said, 'which is more than we are. But aren't they worried about our bill?'

'Not in the least. They asked for payment in advance.'

They were delighted with their little chalet. It was surprisingly spacious and had a most attractive double-bed. It also had a separate shower and an electric point and kettle. The management had even provided little sachets of tea, coffee, milk powder and sugar.

'Let's go in search of a meal, shall we?' Peter suggested. 'They told me that there is a pub in a village near here that does dinners.'

The pub did indeed do excellent dinners, and they greatly enjoyed the atmosphere. It felt almost like being in a private dining-room because it was out of season and only two other people shared a palatial dining-room with them.

'As this is a special treat meal,' said Barbara, 'could we have Nuits St George?'

'We can have what you like,' Peter agreed, 'but it is nearer St Andrews' Day than St George's Day.'

'It may be an odd choice,' said Barbara, 'but I have never chosen the wine before and I am doing so now.'

They walked back and settled down in their little chalet.

'It's almost like a self-contained flat, isn't it?' Barbara said.

The next two or three hours were a completely new experience for her. And she was delighted to find that all was well.

They were to spend two nights at the motel and had not really planned how to spend the day.

'I can now reveal,' said Peter, smiling, 'that I booked two nights just in case things had not gone well at first, but, as they have, we can both really relax today. And thank you very much indeed for last night.'

'It was really to please me, you know,' said Barbara, 'but I'm so glad that you liked it.'

They had a very leisurely breakfast.

'Strangely enough,' said Barbara, 'it has only just occurred to me that, of course, I am not wearing a wedding ring.'

'I don't think that we shall be thrown out on that account,' Peter reassured her. 'Nobody seems to have noticed.'

After breakfast, they drove to the coast. It was a wild and windy day. A long walk along the front was most invigorating and they were glad of their macs – not because it was raining but because the waves were dashing themselves so hard against the sea-wall that Barbara and Peter were often enveloped in spray.

'I do feel happy,' said Peter as they retreated to the town for lunch.

'Me too,' Barbara agreed.

They were somewhat at a loose end in the afternoon and went for a long drive in the car.

'To be honest . . . ,' Peter began.

'Good.' Barbara encouraged him, smiling.

'I'm not very fond of just travelling about in a car.'

'Neither am I,' Barbara agreed, 'but we have no walking

things with us or large scale maps and it is a sight too cold to sit on the beach, so what else could we do this afternoon?'

'That is exactly what I thought.'

'I expect we both felt a bit worked up yesterday afternoon,' said Peter. 'I just feel happy now.'

'You concealed any qualms you had pretty well though.'

'Well, really, it was silly to have had any, I suppose, but it felt very odd writing "Mr and Mrs Johns" in the register. And the receptionist did look a little frightening.'

'Not Mr and Mrs Smith?' Barbara asked.

'No, I hope you didn't want me to do that.'

'No, I would have done what you did. In any case, "Smith" doesn't show much imagination, does it? And it must be very annoying for people who really are called Smith.'

'Here we are again,' said Peter as he halted the car at the entrance to the chalet.

It was surprising how peaceful that evening felt. It was sufficiently cold outside for the well-heated chalet to seem like a refuge, and it was lovely to know that there was nothing to be tested or proved that night. As before, they went down to the local inn for dinner, but a much more leisurely one than on the night before.

The next morning, they drove back to London together.

'That was really lovely, Peter,' Barbara said. 'Now I can really look forward to our wedding without wondering about things.'

'I really would not have "wondered" as you put it, Barbara, but I am very glad that you will feel so much happier. I would have hated it if I had suspected that some lurking worry about that side of things had spoilt the great day for you.'

19

When Barbara was a little girl, she was very fond of a curious legend about a good king who wanted to serve all his subjects as well as he possibly could. It had made a lasting impression on Barbara, who was very fond of good kings who popped up from time to time in the stories of her childhood. According to this particular story, a tremendous number of strings were attached to the king, indeed one for each of his subjects. Whenever any of them was in distress, he could pull his own string and the king would rush to his aid. It was a very charming story, and, now that she was no longer a child, Barbara occasionally wondered whether it was, perhaps, the origin of the phrase 'with strings' and its regrettably more common negative 'without strings'.

It was something of a coincidence that Barbara happened to be thinking about that story when she returned to her flat after the week-end with Peter, because, lying on the mat, awaiting her return, was an envelope with a French stamp on it. Barbara did not recognize the handwriting and opened the envelope with some curiosity. Before reading the letter, she looked at the signature and found, to her surprise, that the letter was from Brenda, from whom she had not heard since the trekking holiday. It was headed with the name and address of a hospital in Brittany.

Dear Barbara,

Perhaps you have forgotten me. We met at the riding place. I feel a bit mean about writing to you now. I have never written before, have I?

Well, I have been very ill and 'came to' in this hospital. I don't know when they are going to let me out!

I suppose you are wondering why I am writing now. Well, I'd like my mother to know that I am still alive. Unfortunately, we have had a bad quarrel and I don't quite know how to set about writing to her. We don't write much anyway.

She lives quite near you.

Am I asking too much for you to go and see her and tell her that I am still around and that, if she'll have me, I'd like to come and see her and be at home for a bit when they let me out of here. Sounds a bit like a prison doesn't it? Well, I'd like to escape anyhow.

The letter went on to give her mother's address.

'Well,' Barbara thought, 'It's funny that I was just thinking about that old favourite story of mine. I'm not a king or even a queen, but somebody has pulled one of my strings so I had better do something about it.'

The prospect of calling on an unknown woman, who might not be particularly pleased to see her, did not fill Barbara with any great joy. Indeed, it was a somewhat daunting idea, and the old, quiet, reserved Barbara, who existed only a few months earlier, simply could not have done it. However, things had turned out so well and happily for her recently that she felt that she must do her best with this extraordinary errand. So, the very next morning, before she had time to have second thoughts, she set off determinedly for Streatham, feeling quite a different kind of nervousness from that which she had several times experienced when setting out on her own adventures.

She found the address without difficulty and, with considerable trepidation, rang the bell. Her mouth felt every bit as dry as it had done when she had stood waiting in the wings before the first performance of 'Zack'. Fortunately, she did not have long to wait. The door was opened by a rather sad-looking woman who, as far as Barbara could guess, was about forty-five years old.

'You don't know me,' Barbara began, 'but I have a message from Brenda.'

'Oh.'

The tone of voice was flat and not encouraging. It was obviously up to Barbara to make the next move.

'I wonder if I could come in for a minute,' she asked. 'It would be easier to talk that way, I think.'

Barbara had never before had to behave in quite so thrusting a fashion. She began to feel like an unwelcome salesman.

'Very well then,' said the woman grudgingly, and she opened the door a fraction wider. Barbara squeezed through. Her unwilling hostess led the way into the front room and pointed, silently, to a chair.

'I met Brenda,' Barbara commenced, 'some months ago on a trekking holiday – horses, you know. I had a letter from her yesterday and she asked me to tell you that she is in France just now.'

'I see,' said Brenda's mother, without displaying any emotion – not even curiosity. This was obviously going to be hard going.

'She is all right, more or less,' Barbara continued, 'but she has been very ill and she is still in a hospital.'

A slight expression of concern floated across the woman's face.

'I see,' she said again.

'When she is better again, she would like to come home for a while,' said Barbara. 'I know it would cheer her up if you say she can, please.'

Brenda's mother was non-committal.

'We'll see,' she said. Not one of the world's great talkers.

Barbara did her level best to get a more generous or even a more definite response, but without success.

'Well,' she said at last, 'thank you for seeing me, Mrs Thomas. I do hope it all comes out right in the end.'

'Perhaps,' was the reserved reply. 'We'll have to see.'

And with that, Barbara had to be content for the time being.

She returned to her flat feeling very disappointed. She had so hoped to be able to write a cheerful letter to her friend, and she was not looking forward to writing now. Family quarrels are dreadful things. How could she possibly write to Brenda, who was generally such a cheerful girl but now so unhappy, that her own mother was being so unhelpful? It was not the sort of letter that she would be pleased to write in normal circumstances, and to address such a letter to a patient in hospital seemed an almost impossible thing to do.

Barbara made herself a pot of tea – one of her few treats in the old days – and sat and thought. She re-read Brenda's letter, and was particularly struck by the phrase: 'I don't know when they are going to let me out of here'. As Brenda had herself written, it made the whole thing sound so like a prison sentence. Barbara had responded to Brenda's string by doing, to the best of her ability, exactly what she had been asked to do, but she still felt the pull of the appeal and she suddenly felt quite sure that Brenda really needed much more than she had thought it reasonable to ask. The letter was a cry for help. Barbara's visit to Brenda's mother had not been a resounding success, and Brenda was still going to be left wondering, in a foreign hospital, when she would be allowed to be free, and what she was going to do after that. What would the good king do next?

Barbara decided to go to Brittany and wondered why she had been so slow to think of that. Perhaps she had been absurdly optimistic about her powers of persuasion with Mrs Thomas. Once she had decided what to do, Barbara moved without delay.

Fortunately, she was able to go immediately to France and was soon speeding on her way to Dover for the short sea route to Calais and then on, by rail, to Rennes via Paris. Rather to her surprise, she enjoyed the journey. There was no point in worrying about the future and, in any case, it felt strangely satisfying to be on an errand of mercy, however things turned out. There was nothing more that she could be doing, and so she could relax. Several hours later, she arrived at the hospital where she explained in her best French why she had come. A Senior Nurse, possibly a Matron or whatever they called them these days, ushered her into a little room and explained that Brenda had had pneumonia but was now well on the way to recovery. She went on to say that the doctors would be happy to discharge her if Barbara could take her back with her to England. Barbara readily agreed and asked for any advice. The nurse explained that Brenda was in no pain but that she was still very weak and that she would still keep falling asleep whenever she had a chance to do so.

Barbara then went into the ward to see Brenda.

Fortunately, she was awake at the time and her eyes shone with such joy and surprise at seeing her friend that Barbara knew straight away how worthwhile her journey had been.

'Oh Barbara,' Brenda said, 'I never once thought that you would come all this way to see me. Or am I dreaming?'

'No, Brenda. This is the real me. And I haven't come just to see you but to take you back with me.'

'They'll let me go? They actually said so?'

'Yes.'

'Fine. When?'

'As soon as we can make proper arrangements. You'll have to have a cabin on the boat.'

'I don't mind how I travel.'

'Well, that's what I have been told by the Matron, or whoever,' Barbara explained.

'But,' said Brenda, looking worried, 'I can't afford that sort of thing. I've got almost no money left.'

'Not to worry,' Barbara said, 'I have.'

'But I can't sponge off you.'

'You can pay me back some time if you insist,' said Barbara. 'No hurry at all.'

'I am pleased to see you,' Brenda said unnecessarily. 'Thank you very, very much.'

'It's a pleasure, really it is,' said Barbara. The excitement was obviously making Brenda sleepy. It seemed an odd result, but Barbara had been warned about that.

'Go to sleep again now,' she said. 'I'll try to make all the arrangements today if I can and see you again tomorrow.'

There was a tourist office in the town, and as it was to be a day crossing, there was no great problem in arranging for a cabin on the boat. And so, the very next morning, Brenda and Barbara set off in a sitting-ambulance for the station.

'But suppose,' said Brenda, 'my mother won't have me?'

'We are not going there first,' Barbara replied. 'We'll spend the first night in my flat.'

The journey back went quite smoothly, including the sea, which was most fortunate. It would have been no fun to deal with Brenda sea-sick as well. Barbara soon got used to the fact that her friend kept falling asleep, but when she was awake, she was very keen to talk, so many things were pent up inside.

'What exactly happened to you?' Barbara asked.

'It's a long story.'

'It's a long journey,' Barbara smiled in reply.

So, with long gaps while she fell peacefully asleep, Brenda related her adventures.

'I came to France for a few days, as I thought,' she said, 'with a man called Jack, but I soon began feeling ill and he got fed up with me.'

'But surely he didn't just get up and go?'

'Oh no, not so suddenly as that. I suppose I just got more and more miserable and we had quite a quarrel. He went after that.'

'He doesn't sound a very trustworthy sort of man.'

Brenda gave a wan smile.

'Trust didn't come into it,' she said.

'But still, it does seem a bit thick,' Barbara insisted. 'If a man takes a girl on a foreign holiday, she doesn't exactly expect to be deserted in the middle of it.'

'Let's be fair to him,' Brenda persisted. 'He came on holiday to enjoy it, and I wasn't exactly a little ray of sunshine.'

'But that wasn't your fault; you were ill.'

'But I didn't tell him that.'

'Why ever not?'

'Two things I suppose. It came on gradually, so I didn't really know myself that I was ill at first and,' here Brenda hesitated, 'I don't go in for excuses.'

'That was very brave of you,' Barbara said.

'I don't think of it like that.'

Soon after waking from one of her frequent short sleeps, Brenda said, 'I wouldn't have asked you to come all the way to France. I couldn't believe it when you turned up.'

'I was glad to.'

'But I'm a bit worried about it.'

'What ever for?'

'I'm not so good at saying what I mean as you are, Barbara, but I'll try. You see, when you go off on jaunts with men that you don't know very well, there is always a risk, so when I do, I think it's my risk, not somebody else's.'

Barbara smiled at her.

'I don't know what you meant by saying that you couldn't explain things properly. That's very clear. But, you see Brenda, you are a friend of mine and I am glad to help.'

'Yes, well, thanks, thanks very much. But you see, I haven't got across what I was really trying to say. It's really this: you are not the sort of girl who would have done what I did – and it's not the first time, either. So why should it be you who comes to the rescue? It ought to be somebody more like me, she might want me to help her some day.'

'What a thing to worry about,' Barbara replied. 'Look, we all need help some time or other. Peter – he's my fiancé – calls it a chain of help.'

'What on earth is a chain of help?'

'Well,' Barbara said, 'I am not so good at explaining things like that as Peter is, but I'll do my best. He believes, and I think he is right, that we should all help where and when we can and not expect something back.'

'But that seems unfair.'

'You are a great one for fairness, aren't you Brenda?' said Barbara approvingly. 'You are sure you want a sort of philosophical discussion?'

'Call it by a fancy name if you want to, Barbara, but I am interested in how people get on together. Who isn't? Why shouldn't I try to help you in return?'

'Because things don't always work out that way. Peter's chain of help, works like this: A helps B, B helps C – but probably she doesn't help A "in return", as you put it.'

'It sounds a bit like algebra,' said Brenda sleepily, 'and I was never any good at that at school.'

'Oh, all right, then,' Barbara continued. 'Sorry if it sounded like maths. All it boils down to is that if you feel under an obligation to me, forget it, but look out for a chance to help somebody else.'

'Well,' said Brenda, 'it's very sweet of you and thanks again, but I still think it's unfair that you are helping me because of a risk that I took, and you wouldn't have.'

'If you had asked me to come here,' Barbara replied after a short pause, 'I might have agreed with you, but you didn't.'

'No, that's true. I never, never thought you would come all the way to France.'

Crossing London on the way to her flat, Barbara had a pleasant surprise. She was always a little afraid of taxi-drivers, they often seemed so unhelpful. Before she got into the cab with Brenda, Barbara explained to the driver that her friend was recovering from a bad illness and asked him to go quite slowly.'

'That's a change,' he said, grinning. 'Most people are in such a 'ell of an 'urry.'

And he drove them very smoothly indeed all the way. Barbara tried to give him an exceptionally generous tip. To her amazement, he gave half of it back to her.

'That's good enough for me, miss,' he said. 'If I can't 'elp someone what's been ill, I'm a poor sort of chap.'

(And Brenda did look so very pale).

That night, Barbara slept on a bed-settee as Brenda was occupying the only bed. The following day, they decided to go to Brenda's mother's house and hope for the best. Mrs Thomas opened the door and a small flicker of surprise and could it be pleasure(?) crossed her face.

'Come in,' she said. 'You're home again are you?'

'Yes, Mum,' Brenda said. 'If you'll have me for a bit.'

Her mother partially reverted to the unhelpful manner that Barbara had experienced on her first call.

'We'll see,' was all she said.

Barbara stayed for a while, hoping to act as a go-between, although it seemed an odd part to play between mother and daughter. After a while, Mrs Thomas began to thaw. For the first time, a smile appeared on her face.

'Stay as long as you like, love,' she said.

20

The day after her return, Barbara rang James Garton to apologize for the long time during which she had been silent, and arranged to see him that afternoon.

'And how have you been getting on, Barbara?' he asked.

'One thing I have been doing is getting engaged to be married.'

'I'm not supposed to say "congratulations", am I? But what I am supposed to say always sounds a bit twee to me – so, please, take it as said; I really am very pleased for you.'

'Thank you.'

'And how about the treasure hunt, if you can bring yourself to talk about such mundane matters?'

Barbara produced her Uncle Tom's letter. James read it with attention.

'So, you are entitled to the fifty thousand pounds now.'

'So I understand,' said Barbara, 'but I would like to do the final clue first.'

'As your great-uncle said in his letter, it's an easy one, but, although I don't need to know about the outdoor activities you have been indulging in, if that is the right word, I should be most interested to hear about them. You seem to have survived.'

'Yes, but it wasn't exactly guaranteed.'

'Whatever do you mean?'

'That was a complicated joke which needs explaining. I did what was called "the General Outdoor Activities" course. There was also a course actually called a "Survival Course". We were amused at the time, especially as they charged more for that.'

'Yes, I see. Did you enjoy it?'

'Most of it very much indeed, thank you.'

James unlocked a drawer, took out a small piece of paper and handed it to Barbara. It was becoming quite a habit by now. How odd that this would be the last. It said:

The Final Clue

The first and the last; but in the original country (W) this time.

Barbara puzzled over this conundrum for some time, but in the end, it dawned on her that the first clue had been about youth hostels and that, therefore, so was the last one. The (W) seemed a bit cryptic but she decided that it must mean West. Youth hostels started in Germany, and West Germany now made very good sense.

Keen now to finish her treasure hunt, Barbara enjoyed planning a route, and she set out for Heidelberg three days later. She was glad that she was not confined to one area because she wanted to see Heidelberg and then to travel by train to Mainz for the start of a walking tour above the Rhine. As she boarded the train for Harwich for the second time, she felt herself to be a seasoned traveller. It was still quite an adventure to be on a boat-train but, this time it seemed less grand than on the first occasion, partly because she had become so much more confident, partly because human beings are so silly that the first occasion for anything is nearly always the best and partly because the trip was, for the first and only time, a prelude to her marriage and therefore less important in itself.

She was a little surprised to find, as the boat pulled away from Parkstone Quay, that she suddenly missed Peter more than ever before. The gradually increasing area of foaming water that was separating her from England seemed also to be separating her from Peter much more dramatically than had the boat-train. How odd it seemed that, after becoming more and more ready for adventures when she had been unattached, she now, for the first time since it had all started, began to wish that it was over. Seriously, though, she did not regret her decision to fulfil the course, it was nice of Uncle Tom to trust her to do so. It was even rather pleasant to think that, on her return, she would not have to produce evidence of her journey.

She had never before set foot in Holland and thoroughly enjoyed the train journey to the Kaldenkirchen frontier, where to her surprise, a powerful-looking girl, complete with pistol in a holster, came down the train to examine passports. She passed the frontier and travelled on to Cologne, Mannheim and Heidelberg. She took more than a day over the whole journey, which she broke for one night at Cologne, where she stayed at an actual hotel. She was not 'bound' to use hostels yet and in a large city they always seemed to her to be out of place, although she was well aware that many hostellers disagreed with her about that. She had time for a leisurely visit to the impressive cathedral before going on to her destination. She was enchanted by the old parts of Heidelberg. She had two all-day walks around that romantic town before taking a train back to Mainz to start her walking tour. She was glad that she had planned her route that way round; each day would take her a bit nearer to Peter.

Once she had thought of that way of looking at it, she was determined to enjoy herself. It would be mean to Uncle Tom to wish this exciting holiday away. She had considerable fun practising her rusty German, and was pleased that some degree of fluency came back to her. At least, it was a help that German is spoken in such a way that, unlike French, you can tell where one word ends and another begins.

The main difference, she discovered, between German hostels and English ones was the early times at which everything happened. She found herself on the road well before nine in the morning – which was an advantage in October when it got dark fairly early. Her walking tour felt like a real-life geography lesson, with the Rhine always below her in the valley, except when she dropped down to a village. She liked the hostel sing-songs in the evening – much more frequent in Germany than at home. It was particularly enjoyable when there were song-books and she could join in herself.

From time to time, she met other English people. They seemed very surprised that she was walking alone and unprotected, all by herself, and although she explained it by what she now thought of as the 'Five Thousand Pounds story', she insisted with such obviously genuine enthusiasm that she was enjoying it that in the end, they believed her. Indeed, on just one occasion, a small group were so determined that she ought to go with them that rather than hurt their feelings, she invented, as an additional condition in the will, that she was bound to walk alone. Actually, she was particularly keen not to be with a chattering group on that occasion, because her path would lead her just above the beautiful Rhine Gorge, with its intriguing medieval castles. She wanted to appreciate all that in quietness and peace.

The weather was superb and, nearly always, the tracks were wide and clear, so that she could enjoy the splendid views without being much distracted by map-reading or by looking down to see where she was putting her feet. It gave her a wonderful feeling of freedom. On two separate occasions, German boys started to chat her up. She did not want that, but felt flattered nevertheless. She was at first a little puzzled that they did not seem to notice her beautiful engagement ring, but it was explained to her that German women wore them on their right hands. It seemed very unfair, to Barbara, that she was offered two 'dates' when she did not need them and had, in the past, so often been left alone when she would have welcomed a friend. She still did not fully realize that because she felt so happy she had become, for that reason alone, not only much more confident but also much more attractive. It was still unfair, and Barbara, like Brenda, very much liked things to be fair.

On just one occasion, not far from Koblenz, she passed a fairly large group of English people walking along one of the paths above the Rhine. She was surprised to discover that the girl who was leading them was much younger than anybody in her party.

'Well,' thought Barbara to herself, 'I can do all sorts of things now that I would not have dreamt of doing last year, but I don't think I could happily lead a party in a foreign country.'

She was just thinking about that when the leader stopped and asked her whether there was a good café in the next village. Barbara replied in English.

'So much for my excellent German,' said the girl, smiling.

'Not at all,' Barbara reassured her, 'I could hear a general buzz of English from your party.'

Barbara walked on, feeling just a little deflated, but she was old enough to realize that some people do find some things easier than others. Also, she was now so generally happy that it did not worry her long that here was something which she could not have done. After all, it was the second thing that she had felt was not for her. She had actually and quite deliberately avoided mountaineering, although accidentally forced into abseiling. However, in some almost miraculous way, Uncle Tom seemed to have foreseen that. She drew some comfort from a remark she had once heard that the more experienced you are in life generally, the more you know what you really cannot do, which explained why nervous and inexperienced people occasionally summoned up courage to do the wrong thing, for them.

Barbara was thus philosophizing to herself when she came to a viewpoint. Well-known tourist areas were much more frequently signposted than they are in England – not just by actual direction posts but by specified viewpoints and even, not infrequently, view-towers. Barbara almost wondered whether the Germans were so used to this that they would deny the existence of a perfectly good view if it was visible only from an unofficial point! She duly stopped to sit on the rustic seat and to admire the view, as 'instructed'. An elderly but energetic gentleman arrived a few minutes later and started complaining about the large number of people who went everywhere by car. Barbara agreed with him to a considerable extent, but was having difficulty in concealing a certain amount of quiet amusement, caused by the fact that she knew an Englishman, of about the same age, who held exactly the same views and who expressed them, although in a different language, in almost exactly the same way. It made wars seem even more absurd and tragic than they usually did to Barbara. It was quite likely, she thought, that the two old gentlemen had spent years firing guns at one another, and they could, in a better purer world, have been the greatest of friends.

Barbara was having a lovely holiday, alone, but not in the least lonely. At every hostel where she stayed, there was a letter from Peter.

When, at the end of her walking tour, she reached Koblenz, she spent a day there just like an ordinary tourist. Barbara subconsciously thought of walkers as superior to 'ordinary tourists'. Like all visitors to Koblenz, she visited the dramatic 'German Corner' where the Moselle flows into the Rhine, to the frequent accompaniment of lengthy hooting whenever a boat was going round a blind corner. Altogether, she had a lovely, leisurely day just sight-seeing and enjoying the sensation of having the day all to herself, as she thought of it. The treasure hunt had been completed, and she herself had changed so much. She was so different now from the diffident and lonely Barbara who had gone every working day so conscientiously to her typewriter and her shorthand notebook.

It was, as she realized herself, perhaps a little surprising that she had decided to have that extra day, and she wondered why she was not rushing back to see her Peter and to wave a metaphorical victory flag in James Garton's office. It was easily explained really. She was very fond of looking forward to nice things, and the very fact that she was postponing for one whole day her next meeting with Peter enhanced, in her view, the prospect of her home-coming. Indeed, she thought of her whole day in Koblenz as what she called a 'Castleday', a peculiar, private word of Barbara's. She had invented the word some years earlier when she had been exceptionally busy. A 'Castleday' was an extra day quite outside the usual run of Sundays to Saturdays. The concept of a 'Castleday' gave her a feeling of boundless leisure, although such a day did not really exist, of course, except in her imagination. On this occasion, it was really a Friday. She had completed what she had set out to do. She and her Uncle Tom had done it together. Wasn't everything quite marvellous!

The following day, as she set out from the hostel for the station, she felt that an exciting part of her life – indeed the first ever such part – had come to an end, but she knew that something quite different and wonderful lay ahead of her. She treated herself to a grand meal on the train as it sped on its way to Flushing. She especially enjoyed crossing the last land frontier into Holland. Barbara had no precise idea to explain why frontiers so appealed to her. She and Peter must some day have a holiday which included actually walking across one. She realized that she did not agree with Ernest Bevin who wanted to go 'where the hell he liked without a passport'. Barbara actually enjoyed the formalities of customs, of passports and, very often, the change of language at a frontier. Even the very word was, to her, poetry.

She enjoyed every minute of the journey back. And reaching Liverpool Street, she rang Peter and they arranged to meet the very next day.

21

As Barbara was, temporarily, a lady of leisure, she suggested getting up early and going by train to meet Peter at Birmingham, but Peter had already arranged to come to London to meet her. She still got up early because it was the first time that Peter would be coming to her flat, and he would be staying until quite late in the evening.

Barbara met Peter at Euston. He had, of course, protested that that was quite unnecessary, but she had made it so clear that she would enjoy doing so that he had agreed with pleasure. It seemed strange to Barbara to go to Euston again, a station that she had used to start the first of her clues at Penrith. How long ago that seemed now!

It was nostalgic to hear the announcer saying, 'Crewe, Preston, Lancaster, Oxenholme, Penrith and Carlisle. Platform 15.'

Peter was flatteringly interested in her flat.

'I have so often tried to visualize it,' he said. 'At last I know what it is really like.'

After a very early lunch, Peter said,

'I don't want to sound like the chairman of a committee, but there are a lot of things for us to arrange before our wedding, so shall we talk about them now?'

'I thought that was why you came up so early.'

'Well, it was mainly because I was so keen to see you, Barbara, but it does also give us a nice long time to discuss things. I needn't go back until quite late. You asked about that on the phone for some reason.'

'We'll come back to that later,' Barbara smiled, 'but the rest of the "agenda" you can arrange.'

'Well then, first of all, the date of our wedding.'

'All I shall want on that,' Barbara replied, 'is a day when

Edna can come – and my mother.'

'Talking of mothers, mine would, I know, like it to be a white wedding at our parish church – but, before you answer that,' Peter continued quickly, 'if you don't want that, it would be quite all right.'

'I would be very happy with it. Edna is often on at me for not going to church more often than I do. So, no problem there.'

'The honeymoon presents a problem,' Peter said, but he looked so unworried about it that Barbara realized that the 'problem' was little more than a joke.

'What is so problematical about it?'

'Just that you have been all over the place recently such a lot that I wonder where you would most like to go to as a treat.'

'I'll think about it, unless there's somewhere you have set your heart on?'

'No.'

After a pause, Peter said,

'I'm glad that I made it so clear right at the start that we will more or less have to live with my mother. I would have hated to spring that on you as a hidden condition, as it were.'

'Oh yes, Peter,' said Barbara demurely, 'you made that quite plain.'

There was something in her tone of voice that made Peter realize that she had more to say, but he could not begin to guess what it was.

'You really don't mind?'

'No,' said Barbara. And, again, there was such an odd mixture of doubt, and was it amusement(?) in her voice that Peter said,

'I have been worried about it actually. I expect you would have preferred a house of our own.'

'Wouldn't you?'

'Well, yes, but I don't see how we can.'

'Fortunately,' said Barbara, and this time there was no doubt whatever about the amusement in her voice, 'I can wave a wand and the problem is solved.'

Peter looked nonplussed, as well he might.

'You remember the time when your mother arranged to talk to me alone?'

'Yes. I did wonder what that was all about.'

'It was about this. She would actually like us to have our own house, not too far away.'

'She would? She was not just saying so?'

'She meant it all right.'

'But I thought,' said Peter, sounding somewhat hurt, 'that she really wanted me around.'

'Of course she did,' and there was no amusement in Barbara's voice this time. 'She made everything very clear to me. So long as you are a bachelor, she was delighted, but she would feel that she was imposing on you if you went on living there after we are married, and she would actually not like it then. Nobody enjoys feeling guilty, you know.'

'Well,' said Peter in a surprised tone, 'that's all right, then.'

'You don't sound very pleased.'

'I am pleased, really; it is just that this has come as such a surprise.'

'Let's have some mid-morning coffee,' said Barbara. It seemed a good time for a break.

'So,' Peter resumed, 'you have finished the last of your gallivants. Has your solicitor paid over the prize?'

'No, I'll be seeing him tomorrow.'

'I've been thinking while you were making the coffee.'

'Yes?'

'Five thousand is just the right amount,' said Peter. 'I would have been sorry if it had been any more.'

'Oh!'

'Yes, Barbara,' said Peter. 'You see, I have a good job and I have never had any special need to spend a lot of money. I can easily buy our house, and so your money can be your very own to do exactly what you like with.'

'But,' said Barbara, 'we are getting married, aren't we? Wouldn't you like some help with buying the house or the furniture or anything?'

'No, no,' said Peter emphatically. 'I suppose it's odd, but like many men, I think, I would like to feel that I am supporting my wife. Or is that an "old hat" idea?'

'No,' said Barbara, after a slight pause which she hoped Peter had not noticed. 'That's fine.'

And, although she did not honestly think that it was 'fine'

she managed to conceal any sound of disappointment in her voice.

'Well that's settled then,' Peter said.

'Barbara,' he continued a few seconds later, 'you talked about waving a wand. I'm a little worried about the "and they lived happily ever after" idea.'

'I am not worried in the least,' Barbara reassured him. 'I don't suppose we shall.'

'What ever do you mean?'

'I know exactly what I mean, but it may take a bit of explaining. Do you know the story of Polycrates' ring?'

'No.'

'Polycrates was a very rich king, so rich that he could have everything that he wanted, and he thought he was perfectly happy, But, one day, he met a wise man who told him nobody was allowed to be perfectly happy for ever. Polycrates asked him what he should do about it. The wise man told him to throw away his most treasured possession. So, that very day, Polycrates threw a wonderful golden ring into the river. That evening, at supper, a large fish was served in a silver dish and, as the servant cut the fish, out fell Polycrates' golden ring. "There is no help for you," cried the wise man, "because you cannot be happy for ever. The Fates must have something in store that you cannot avoid".'

'And what,' Peter asked, 'am I to make of that impressive tale?'

'Certainly not to take it literally,' Barbara replied, 'but I do think that there is a lot of truth in it. I shall feel very, very happy, Peter, if we can both go ahead from, as the Americans say, here on out, knowing that everything will not be perfect but that we shall deal with it together when things go wrong.'

Peter stood up and kissed Barbara's hair.

'What a lovely way of putting it,' he said. 'Of course, I agree.'

They sat in happy silence for several minutes.

'When you told the Polycrates story so beautifully,' Peter resumed, 'I could not help but daydream, if a man is allowed to do that, about our having children.'

'Me too, but what made you think of that just then?'

'Nothing to do with that particular story, but I visualized

you telling fairy tales to them.'

'Let's hope so, Peter.'

After another short silence, Peter said, 'That, then, is the finish of the agenda.'

'Very unusual agenda.'

'What's wrong with it – or do I mean them?'

'What about "Any Other Business"?'

'Of course,' Peter agreed. 'Sorry. I should have thought of that. Does the committee have any other business?'

'The committee,' said Barbara, echoing the word, 'has two further items to discuss.'

'And the first is?'

'Can you get me an elementary text-book on mechanical engineering?'

'A what?'

'At the risk of sounding pert,' Barbara answered, 'you heard.'

'Indeed I did, but what on earth do you want that for?'

'You told me, at Spa, that you were a mechanical engineer.'

'Yes.'

Peter was still baffled.

'Well, I want to know something about what you do all day.'

'But you might not find it exactly enthralling.'

'I want to know a bit about it because it is your job,' said Barbara simply.

'Thank you, Barbara, I'll buy one tomorrow.'

And then, quite unexpectedly, he laughed. Barbara had never before seen him so spontaneously amused.

'What is so funny?'

'I was wondering whether I ought first to buy a stick-on beard and dark glasses. What are any of my professional colleagues going to think if a rumour reaches them that I am in desperate need of an elementary book on mechanical engineering?'

Barbara saw the point and laughed with him.

'There is still the second item.'

'Oh yes. sorry.'

'You have still got to like Edna, remember?'

'I do indeed remember and I am sure I shall.'

'Well, you can do it this evening, she's coming here for an early dinner.'

'So that is why you wanted to know if I could stay late.'

'Yes, but it may not be quite as important as I first thought that you should like her. She is bringing somebody with her, and he is not called Donald.'

'Is there any special reason why he should be called Donald?' Peter asked quizzically. 'Lots of men are not called Donald. It may or may not have escaped your notice that I am not called Donald.'

'No, but, you see, the only man that Edna has ever mentioned before was called Donald. She seems to be branching out.'

22

When Peter, Edna and her friend had gone, Barbara sat down to think.

It had not occurred to her, until that very day, that in order not to show off she had told everybody, including Peter himself, that the legacy was of five thousand, and not fifty thousand pounds. It now seemed to her that it would have to stay that way.

Clearly, as Peter had so innocently revealed, he would not have proposed to a rich girl and, alas, it seemed that he would not feel very happy if Barbara had a lot of money of her own. Barbara went over and over the problem in her mind. Peter's attitude did not make a great deal of sense to her, but she very much loved him and the last thing she wished to do was to disappoint him. Still, she could not quite make up her mind what was the best thing to do. Peter's view had come as a complete surprise to her. True, she had heard of marriages which had foundered simply because the wife had had much more money or a much better job than her husband. Certainly the picture which she had in her mind of her marriage to Peter seemed perfect to her. Very well then, it must remain perfect. Barbara was pleasantly surprised to find how remarkably unattached to money she was.

Now that she had made up her mind, she went happily and peacefully to bed. The next morning, she rang James Garton and went to see him. He listened, as always, with great interest to her news, and then he said,

'Well that's it then. I'll write out the cheque now. Congratulations.'

'Not too fast please,' said Barbara. 'There is something I must discuss with you first.'

'I can't imagine what there is to discuss,' James replied,

smiling. 'I have never before met anybody who wanted to put anything between themselves and a cheque for fifty thousand pounds.'

'Well, you have now.'

'So it seems.' James sounded mystified. 'Would you explain, please.'

'Certainly. But what I have to say is confidential.'

'Of course.'

'Even from my fiancé.'

James could not entirely conceal a look of surprise. Barbara seemed to him to be a most unlikely person to have guilty secrets.

'Certainly,' he said.

'Like everybody else – I didn't want to boast you see – Peter thinks that the legacy is only five thousand pounds.'

'So?'

'Quite by accident, he made it clear last night that he would not like it to be more than that.'

'But it is more than that.'

'I know, but,' said Barbara, with a slightly mischievous smile. 'Isn't there something about teeth? I seem to have read it somewhere.'

James began to wonder if success had turned Barbara's brain.

'Teeth?' he echoed.

At their first meeting, it had been Barbara who had done the echoing.

'Despite them, or something like that, I am not actually bound to accept the whole amount, am I?'

'Well, no. No, indeed but this is a great surprise. What do you want me to do?'

'I've thought about it for hours and I have come to the conclusion that I'll take the five thousand with pleasure if we can work out some sort of scheme for the remaining forty-five thousand.'

'What sort of scheme do you have in mind?'

'I don't know myself exactly, but I've got some ideas. That is what I want to talk over with you. You see, I have done so well out of all my adventures – not just the money but all my fun and feeling so different and happy – that I am wondering whether we could set up some sort of trust, or whatever, so that other people could have the same lovely chance that I had.'

'We could set up a trust,' James agreed, 'but I would like a little time to think about the details.'

'So shall I,' Barbara said.

'In the meantime, of course, you are still personally entitled to the whole fifty thousand. Here is a cheque for five thousand now, and we will both give the matter some further thought. Can you see me a week from now?'

'Certainly.'

'Just one other thing, Barbara. Everything you tell me is confidential, but the will is a public document, you know.'

'I'm not in the least worried about that,' said Barbara. 'Peter is not the sort of person who would want to read the will.'

23

A few days later, Peter had arranged to come to London to see Barbara for the last time before the wedding. He was not due to arrive until about lunchtime, so Barbara had nothing special to do in the morning. It was, therefore, an extra treat to receive a letter from Juliet.

My dear Barbara,

You will be pleased to know that all is well again.
Just the other day, everything seemed suddenly to click back into place and I felt quite all right again. I can't quite describe it. I don't know how to thank you for all you did for me. I don't think I could have got started again all by myself.
So really there is no need for you to come to see me again. I have just re-read what I have written and it sounds rude. It wasn't meant to. Of course, I'd love to see you again, but just as a normal person would want to see you again. All clear?

Thanks again,

Love,

Juliet.

What a lovely beginning to a lovely day.

Peter arrived for lunch and they spent a lot of time in the afternoon making final plans for the wedding.

When all the i's had been dotted and the t's crossed, Barbara said,

'The evening with Edna went just as I had hoped.'

'Well, I had no difficulty in complying with your

instructions to like her.'

'I was so glad you liked her really. And her friend seemed very nice.'

In the evening, Barbara had agreed to be educated, as she put it. She had been a little bothered that Peter was musical and she was not. She so wanted to share all his interests, which, as it now appeared, did not, somewhat to her relief, include model railways. Peter had booked for them two really good seats to see a performance of a grand opera, Handel's *Tamburlaine*. Barbara was determined to enjoy it if she possibly could.

After the show, Peter said,

'I really want to know what you thought about it, Barbara. Please don't just say you liked it if you didn't.'

'I don't think you will mind my honest answer,' said Barbara, 'because I have had a most enjoyable evening.'

'Good. But what are the reservations?'

'Peter,' said Barbara enthusiastically, 'that's great. I think that it matters much more that you could tell I had reservations than that I should fully appreciate opera, don't you?'

'I do indeed,' Peter answered, 'but I would still like to know what they are.'

'There are two of them. The first is that I don't begin to understand why the part of Tamburlaine himself was played by a counter-tenor. I don't want to be rude but, to my untrained ear, it sounded like a girl singing. Whatever else Tamburlaine may have been, he was most certainly not a girl.'

'It was the tradition in Handel's own day, for reasons we needn't go into,' Peter replied. 'Did it spoil it for you?'

'At first. Then, I realized I liked his voice as a voice, provided that I dissociated it from the part – from the character of Tamburlaine, I mean.'

'Good. Yes. And your other criticism?'

'It is hardly fair to Handel to call my untutored views a "criticism",' said Barbara, 'I preferred your word "reservation".'

'Point taken,' Peter agreed. 'What was it anyway?'

'I appreciate,' said Barbara, 'that the music is pleasantly repetitive but I don't quite see why the words have to be so repetitive too.'

'Again, just tradition, I think.'

'Well, I'm not used to it yet,' Barbara said, 'but I suppose it must be nice to say something so many times if you really like the idea behind the words.'

'Such as?'

'Well, I can't quote from the opera; but fancy my saying,

>*We're* to be married next month.
>We're *to be* married next month.
>We're to be *married* next month.
>We're to be married *next month*.

It makes me feel like a teenager.'

'Like a teenager or not,' Peter argued, 'it sounds enthusiastic. I'll have you composing an opera if you are not very careful.'

24

The following afternoon it occurred to Barbara that it would be nice to go to see her friend Anne in her old office. One of the really good things about being happy was that she wanted to spread it around. It seemed very odd to her to set off for the City for the first time ever without actually going to work there. As she passed St Paul's and made her way along some of the curiously narrow streets which abound in the City of London, Barbara realized for the first time how attractive they were. Always before, she had been duty-bound and had not had the time, nor perhaps the inclination to gaze at the unique beauty of the City, enhanced, rather than spoilt by the throngs of busy people hurrying along without seeing anything. And what lovely names some of the streets had: Playhouse Yard, Carter Lane, Whitefriars Street, Shoe Lane, Cloth Fair, and Paternoster Row – no such thing as a common 'Road'. Quite a poem in itself.

In one way, her visit to the old office was not a success. She had never except perhaps just before the end, been particularly well liked there. Barbara was very sensitive to atmosphere, and she detected a mixture of envy and of surprise that she had not only escaped into the freedom of the wide world but that she had also somehow acquired her beautiful engagement ring. Who would have wanted to marry the old Barbara they had known? The staff did not really believe in or accept their 'ugly duckling' and Barbara began to feel that her visit was a mistake. She wondered whether everybody thought that she was showing off – the very last thing that she ever wanted to do. Fortunately there was one clear exception, which saved the day for her. Anne seemed really pleased to see her and, to Barbara's surprise, asked so many detailed questions about her travels that she, quite naturally, invited Anne to her flat the following evening. As she did so, Barbara realized that spontaneity was a quality which she had gained in the last few months. It was all part of being really and truly alive. Insecure people are never spontaneous, it is too dangerous.

Barbara had great fun in preparing a really nice little dinner for Anne. It was only since she had left her regular nine-to-five job that she had developed an interest in cookery, and then only when she had invited a friend to come and see her.

Anne arrived on time; she would. Barbara was touched to notice that she had made an almost pathetic, but successful, attempt to look very nice for her evening out. A rarity perhaps? Anne was about the same age as Barbara and had no great pretensions to beauty, but then, of course, neither, in the old days, had Barbara.

They had never been great friends, but at least they were, to some extent, on the same wavelength, and that had been something in so small an office. The meal started with a homemade vegetable soup – Barbara had had all day to prepare – and then there was a delicious casserole, followed by a trifle with real cream. Much to Barbara's astonishment and pleasure, Anne accepted a second helping of the casserole with obvious alacrity and pleasure.

'I do hope I'm not being greedy,' said Anne in response, Barbara feared, to a slight expression of surprise that must have flitted across her face.

'It's lovely to have it appreciated,' she said. 'I've only recently got interested in cookery, so I'm very flattered.'

'Well, I certainly do appreciate this,' Anne said. 'You see, I haven't . . . I haven't had a real treat for a long time.'

As she said that, her voice broke just a little and, to her consternation, a solitary tear rolled down her cheek. She hastily wiped it away, not before Barbara had seen it, and made a valiant attempt to switch the conversation to some other topic.

By now, Barbara was not only much more confident but also much more sympathetic to other people than she had been in the old days, when she would have gone along with Anne's courageous effort to talk about something else instead.

'There is no need to hide whatever it is from me, Anne,' said

Barbara. 'Tell me all about it.'

Anne did not reply immediately.

'It's nothing to worry about really,' she said at last. 'You see, I suddenly realized, when you left us, that I was very fed up and that I was going nowhere. I couldn't see what I could possibly do about it, and then I thought of what had happened to you.'

'Yes?'

'Well, I don't have any rich great-uncles – I don't think so anyway, so I decided to do it by myself.'

She paused. Anne was not the kind of person who could have engineered a dramatic pause, but it was made dramatic by her sincerity.

'I'm saving up,' Anne continued, 'and when I've got two thousand pounds, I'll risk packing it in for a bit and go for some holidays – and things,' she added lamely.

'You mean,' Barbara asked, 'that that is why you have been having no treats.'

'Yes, indeed it is. I'm really saving very hard.'

Barbara then realized that Anne had been overdoing things; the poor girl was half starved.

'Well,' she said, 'that's great, but please go on enjoying your treat now. I sound a bit conceited about my cooking, don't I? But you do seem to like my little dinner.'

When they were sitting in front of the fire with their coffee, Barbara said,

'Tell me to mind my own business if you want to, but how far have you got towards your two thousand?'

'Four hundred and twenty-three pounds so far,' said Anne, with an odd mixture of pride and slight disappointment. 'The target does seem a bit out of reach, but it's getting nearer every week.'

'Well,' said Barbara cryptically, 'I am not about to offer you two thousand pounds.'

But her secret smile belied the otherwise abrupt effect of her words.

'Of course not,' Anne expostulated. 'I wouldn't have told you if you hadn't asked, and I wouldn't have told you even then if I had thought you were going to offer me money.'

Anne sounded quite horrified.

'Well I am,' said Barbara. 'Fifteen hundred and seventy-seven pounds.'

As Barbara had hoped, Anne did not immediately take in the significance of the exact amount, so she could not react negatively on the spot.

'But I can't take money from you,' Anne expostulated.

'I don't see why not. I took it from Uncle Tom.'

'But he was dead.'

'Would you rather I was dead?'

'What a dreadful idea. Of course I wouldn't.'

'Well then?'

'No, sorry,' said Anne. 'It's very sweet of you but I couldn't really.'

Barbara suddenly saw the way out. She had not yet actually set up a trust, but it was in preparation. Why should she not advance things a little?

'It won't exactly be a present from me,' Barbara said. 'I am a trustee of part of Uncle Tom's estate.'

'I don't know anything about law. What is that supposed to mean?'

'It means,' said Barbara, 'that there is a fund, much bigger than sixteen hundred pounds, that I can appoint – I think that that's the correct legal word – to other people.'

Barbara was pleased that she had found a way of putting it that avoided the word 'gift'.

Anne looked stunned.

'You really could?' she asked, 'and you really would, for me?'

'I would love to.'

'I can hardly believe it,' said Anne.

'Neither could I when it happened to me,' Barbara agreed.

'I thought I just had a dream to play with,' said Anne, 'and now it's coming true.'

Barbara remembered how she herself had thought, so many months ago, that she had dreamt her own good luck. She had been reassured when she had seen the cheque. It was very unlikely that Anne would think it odd that one trustee could sign a cheque, so Barbara went to a drawer and made out a cheque. The money for the future trust had already been put into her name.

'It was taking such a time to scrape together my two

thousand,' said Anne, after profuse expressions of thanks for the cheque, 'that I haven't got round to making any real plans. I don't know where to start.'

'Well,' said Barbara, 'the first thing I did was to walk to a tube station.'

'Why a tube station?'

'I had to go to London to get some proper walking clothes,' Barbara explained, 'but I was very pleased with what it said on the tube ticket. It felt like being let out of prison.'

'And what did it say?'

'Forward from Clapham South,' said Barbara.

St. Antholin's Lectureship Charity Lectures

In or about 1559 the parish of St. Antholin, now absorbed into what is the parish of St Mary-le-Bow in Cheapside and St Mary Aldermanbury, within the Cordwainer's Ward in the City of London, came into the possession of certain estates known as the 'Lecturer's Estates.' These were, it is believed, purchased with funds collected at or shortly after the date of the Reformation for the endowment of lectures, mid-week sermons or talks by Puritan preachers.

Over the centuries the funds were not always used for the stated purpose, and in the first part of the nineteenth century a scheme was drawn up which revivified the lectureship, which was to consist of forty lectures to be given three times a year on the "Puritan School of Divinity", the lecturer to receive one guinea per lecture. A further onerous requirement was that the lecturer had to be a beneficed Anglican, living within one mile of the Mansion House in the City of London.

Under such conditions the lectureship fell into disuse a long time ago, and it was not until 1987 that moves were put in hand with the Charity Commissioners to update the scheme. The first lecture under the new scheme was given in 1991.

Trustees: The Reverend W.T. Taylor
The Reverend Dr. M.E. Burkill
The Reverend Dr. L. Gatiss

St Antholin's Lectureship Charity Lectures

1991   J.I.Packer, *A Man for All Ministries: Richard Baxter 1651-1691*.
1992   Geoffrey Cox, *The Recovery and Renewal of the Local Church: the Puritan Vision*.
1993   Alister E. McGrath, *Evangelical Spirituality – Past Glories – Present Hopes – Future Possibilities*.
1994   Gavin J. McGrath, *'But We Preach Christ Crucified': The Cross of Christ in the Pastoral Theology of John Owen*.
1995   Peter Jensen, *Using the Shield of Faith – Puritan Attitudes to Combat with Satan*.
1996   J.I.Packer, *An Anglican to Remember – William Perkins: Puritan Popularizer*.
1997   Bruce Winter, *Pilgrim's Progress and Contemporary Evangelical Piety*.
1998   Peter Adam, *A Church 'Halfly Reformed' – the Puritan Dilemma*.
1999   J.I.Packer, *The Pilgrim's Principles: John Bunyan Revisited*.
2000   Ashley Null, *Conversion to Communion: Thomas Cranmer on a Favourite Puritan Theme*.
2001   Peter Adam, *Word and Spirit: The Puritan-Quaker Debate*.
2002   Wallace Benn, *Usher on Bishops: A Reforming Ecclesiology*.
2003   Peter Ackroyd, *Strangers to Correction: Christian Discipline and the English Reformation*.
2004   David Field, *'Decalogue' Dod and his Seventeenth Century Bestseller: A Four Hundredth Anniversary Appreciation*.
2005   Chad B. Van Dixhoorn, *A Puritan Theology of Preaching*.
2006   Peter Adam, *'To Bring Men to Heaven by Preaching' – John Donne's Evangelistic Sermons*.
2007   Tony Baker, *1807 – 2007: John Newton and the Twenty-first Century*.
2008   Lee Gatiss, *From Life's First Cry: John Owen on Infant Baptism and Infant Salvation*.
2009   Andrew Atherstone, *Evangelical Mission and Anglican Church Order: Charles Simeon Reconsidered*
2010   David Holloway, *Re-establishing the Christian Faith – and the Public Theology Deficit*.
2011   Andrew Cinnamond, *What matters in reforming the Church? Puritan Grievances under Elizabeth I*.
2012   Peter Adam, *Gospel Trials in 1662: To stay or to go?*
2013   Lee Gatiss, *Edmund Grindal – The Preacher's Archbishop*
2014   Lee Gatiss, *"Strangely Warmed" – Whitefield, Toplady, Simeon and Wesley's Arminian Campaigns*
2015   Richard Turnbull, *Transformed Heart, Transforming Church: The Countess of Huntingdon's Connexion*

St Antholin's Lectureship Charity Lectures

2016   Martyn Cowan, *Lessons from the Preaching of John Owen (1616–1683)*

ed. Lee Gatiss, *Pilgrims, Warriors, and Servants: Puritan Wisdom for Today's Church: St Antholin lectures 1991-2000*

ed. Lee Gatiss, *Preachers, Pastors, and Ambassadors: Puritan Wisdom for Today's Church: St Antholin Lectures 2001-2010*